Hatshepsut:
The Pharaoh's Daughter

Hatshepsut:
The Pharaoh's Daughter

by

Leslie Howe

Drinian Press/
Huron, Ohio

Cover illustration by Constance Baikie.

Drinian Press LLC
PO Box 63
Huron, Ohio 44839

Online at www.DrinianPress.com.

Library of Congress Control Number: 2015934382

ISBN-10: 1-941929-01-X

ISBN-13: 978-1-941929-01-8

Printed in the United States of America

In honor of
Meredith Kline, my seminary professor, who started me thinking about Pharaoh's daughter and Constance Baikie, a minister's wife from Scotland, who painted some of the illustrations in this book one hundred years before it was written. Many thanks also to my husband, Rev. David Howe.

Contents

Background Information

About Names

Ancient kings and queens had many titles and names. These may have been assigned at strategic events during the life of the individual. Kings often have a more formal name upon succession to the throne. In most instances I have used the name that has come down through history for various characters. I am not certain when each name was actually adopted. In some cases I have made up nicknames to facilitate the story.

About Calendars

Before Christ there was no universal dating system. Every nation had its own reference points. Events were documented by naming the ruler who was in power. This scheme has its own problems because one king did not necessarily come to power immediately upon the death of his predecessor. In many instances a wise ruler would form a co-regency with the person he wanted to rule upon his death so that the dates of various rulers could overlap.

Most ancient cultures made some reference to lunar changes. This makes it possible to track months more easily than years. The Hebrews followed a seven-day week, a lunar month of twenty-nine or thirty days. Dates were counted from the new moon. When the seasons got out of alignment they added another month. Egypt followed a different system. They had a ten-day cycle of 8 days of work and two days of rest and a month of thirty days; four months to a season and three seasons to a year. Five festival days completed the pattern. The demarcations of seasons depended on the workings of the Nile. There were three seasons: Inundation, Growth and Harvest. These variations make it impossible to align dates perfectly. All such correlations must be approximate.

About North and South

The Nile river flows from central Africa to the Mediterranean Sea. The Southern part of the Nile is in the mountains; the Northern part ends at sea level. So, Upper Egypt is South and Lower Egypt is North.

About Dates

Readers of the Bible are often eager to align the stories of the Bible with the history of other nations. In the book of Exodus, the Hebrews are forced to build the store cities of Pithom and Rameses. The assumption is often made that the Pharaoh of that time must therefore be Rameses II. In fact, the Biblical text never calls the Pharaoh Rameses and since both Hebrew and Egyptian written languages omit vowels, this identification is not necessarily certain. The title "Pharaoh's daughter" has been identified with Hatshepsut for millennia. There are numbers in the Biblical account that can be used to calculate the approximate date of the Exodus. Critics of such dating are quick to state that numbers are the most susceptible to errors in the copying of manuscripts because errors in that realm cannot be recognized by context. There are three such calculations where numbers are given in the Scriptures that reference the Exodus and, though granted they may be interdependent, they all indicated a date of about 1440 BC for the Exodus. This makes the whole Moses saga occur during the time when all the Pharaohs had names with Moses (Egyptian for "child") in them.

I Kings 6:1 says, "...in the four hundred and eightieth year after the children of Israel were come out of the land of Egypt, in the fourth year of Solomon's reign over Israel, in the month Zif, which is the second month, that he began to build the house of the LORD."The date for Solomon's reign is known to be approximately 960 BC. Add to that the years mentioned in this text,480, and the calculated date of the Exodus is 1440 BC as stated above. Judges 11:26 states that at the time of the Judge Jephthah, Israel had been in the land for 300 years also confirming the Biblical timeline. Acts13:19 states that the period of Judges lasted for 450 years. If dates are taken at face value then the pre-Exodus narrative described here took place during the Eighteenth Dynasty. The Pharaohs were as follows:

Amosis (great-grandfather of Hatshepsut)
Amenhotep (grandfather of Hatshepsut)
Thutmoses I, (father of Hatshepsut)
Thutmoses II, (husband of Hatshepsut)
Thutmoses III, (step-son of Hatshepsut, she was his regent)
Amenhotep II (son of Thutmoses III)

Historical Setting and Characters

Pharaohs from Earlier dynasties	King Zoser his servant: Imhotep King Pepi (ruled for 90 years)

This story begins in the Eighteenth Dynasty, a time when Egypt's powers are growing after an earlier period of decline when the kingdom was ruled by foreign powers and the country was divided into Northern and Southern Kingdoms

Tao, The Brave	(drove out foreign rulers)
Amosis	(His wife was called the Great Mother. She was the daughter of Tao and mother to Amenhotep.)
Amenhotep	(Hatshepsut's grandfather whom she called "Pepi")
Thutmoses I	(Hatshepsut's father who was married to the daughter of Amenhotep)
Thutmoses II	(Husband of Hatshepsut, son of Thutmoses I His nickname is Twoey in this book.)
Thutmoses III	(Son of Thutmoses II and Isis who married "Beauty," the daughter of Hatshepsut.)
Amenhotep II	(Hatshepsut's grandson)
Pharaohs after story	Thutmoses IV Amenhotep III Amenhotep IV Akhenaten (known for monotheism)

Architects: Ineni, Senenmut
Soldier: Ramose (son of Pharaoh Amosis)
Biblical names: Jocobed, Aaron, Miriam, Amram, Puah, Shiphrah, Jethro, Zipporah, Gershom, Eliezer, Bezaleel and Aholiab

Hatshepsut:
The Pharaoh's Daughter

"Chasing the Sun"
(photo credit:: Elisabeth Howe)

Chapter 1:
Sun Chase

The hard clay road shot forward, like an arrow. In the far distance it appeared to take a left turn to the West. The bright green foliage on either side of the road was transformed into luminescence by the brilliant gold of the sky that made the under sides of the clouds look like molten steel. The river paralleling the road reflected all.

Here and there doors began to open. Small groups of young and old congregated along the side of the road. Snatches of conversation could be heard. "I wonder. Will she ride tonight?" "I think she will come." "The old king is back; he can never say 'No' to her." "It's such a beautiful night." Speculation turned to certainty with the clip-clop sound of horse hoofs coming faster and faster from the south. Soon they came into sight. A lone driver, tall and strong though wrinkled and tanned by the sun, held the reins. Beside him stood a young girl with her left arm stretched behind her grandfather and her right held out in front as if to increase the speed of the chariot. Her princess braid danced wildly around her head as they flew by. The child's laughter was reflected in the faces of the watchers. "She'll stop on the way back." "I'll see if there are any flowers to give her." "Little dear, our Pharaoh's daughter, so sad about her older brother and sister."

The chariot sped forward, but came to a stop around the bend in the road. Grandfather and child watched the last of the sunset over the mountains to the west of the Nile. "Tell me a story, Pepi. Tell me of Tao, The Brave. It's my favorite."

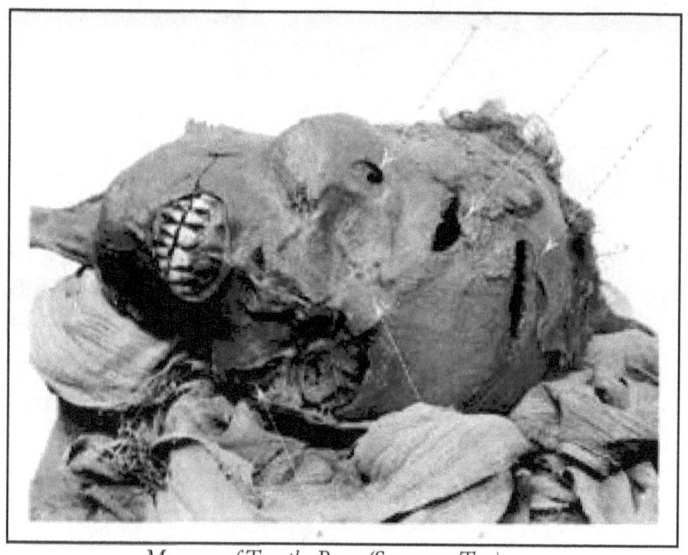

Mummy of Tao the Brave(Seqenerre Tao)

"My grandfather, your great-great-grandfather was a brave soldier. Upper and Lower Egypt had been divided. He fought fearlessly to gain control of Lower Egypt and he won. His body took many blows, but he never stopped fighting. His bravery gave his men great strength, and they drove the Hyksos kings from the land. His son Amosis also fought and managed to unite the land. Now we have a chance to restore

Egypt to the former glory of the Old Kingdom. Never again will it be divided."

"Pepi, you're not telling it right! You're supposed to start, 'The East is for the living. The West is for the dead. The Nile will bring new life!'"

The old man laughed. "Very well. The East is for the living. The West is for the dead. The life-giving Nile lies between. Our houses are on the East bank of the Nile. The West is set aside for the bodies of the dead. Someday the Nile will rise and those whom Ma'at deems worthy, those who are true and good will have their body parts gathered together to new life. Osiris' body was cut and scattered and Isis traveled around in a boat and gathered the pieces together, and the Nile gave him back his life. Our father Tao's body was broken. It was cut in so many places that the embalmers had trouble binding the mummy together. Everyone knows he was just and honest and brave. The Nile will have no trouble putting his body back together. Now he lives among the gods and is one of the gods himself. His blood flows in the lives of all the Pharaohs of Egypt."

"Does it flow in mine, grandfather?"

"Yes, you, my child, are the Daughter of the gods. You will be the Wife of the gods and the Mother of the gods."

"Isn't the Great Mother, god's wife of Amon, the daughter of Tao?"

"She is. She was a great warrior herself, my mother. I was seven, just about your age, when my father, her husband, the great Amosis died and my brother became Pharaoh. Then he died, and I was too young to really serve as Pharaoh so my mother ruled as regent. When I became older, we ruled together, and when she thought I was ready, she turned everything over to me. It was a good idea, that sharing of the power. It helped the people in the time of uncertainty. They knew no enemy could take advantage of her. It made the transition much better, and we agreed on what needed to be done. She had such good ideas. The arts have flourished because of The Place of Truth, Set Ma'at. It was her idea. I agreed that there be a center where the gifted are taught plaster crafts, carving, and tomb embellishment. She wanted a place where the young are taught to read and write and illustrate copies of all the great books. At the time I didn't really understand what it would do for the kingdom, but I am beginning to. What would the monuments in the temple complex be without them? Ineni, the great architect, teaches there. Senenmut, the son of my mother's brother Ramose, is the most skilled of the young workers. You've seen my mother's gold scarab necklace and the memorials of your father's victories. They are beautifully done. What a wise woman, my mother."

"She is old now, though. Will she move to the West soon, Pepi? Do you know why I call you *Pepi*? In the stories you told me, he was the Pharaoh who lived for such a long time. I want you to live a long time, too and chase the sun with me every day. That's why I like to call you *Pepi*. The dead must laugh when they see us coming. Will the Great Mother laugh when we chase the sun?"

"Yes, I think she will. Your mother will be chasing me if we don't return to the palace soon."

"But we must stop and see the Rekhyt, my people. They expect me!"

"Very well," he said.

Hatshepsut: The Pharaoh's Daughter

Pharaoh Amenhotep, called Pepi by Hatshepsut

Only Hatshepsut called him *Pepi*, but he was the Pharoah Amenhotep. He tugged the horse's reins to turn the chariot back South along the road. When they reached the small houses at the end of the temple complex, he stopped and the girl stepped out off the chariot, accepting the help of the closest of her people. He watched in the fading light as she paused at every group of bystanders. She gratefully accepted their flowers as precious gifts; she smiled, bowed, and hugged everyone.

Thutmoses with his wife and
oldest daughter (K. R. Lepsius)

When she turned her attention toward her subjects, the old Pharaoh thought about his granddaughter's words. She called him *Pepi*, and he didn't doubt that she meant it in an endearing way, but the name stabbed at his heart. The Pharoah called *Pepi* had ruled for ninety years and, at his death, the kingdom fell apart because he had not made preparation for a successor. Did he think he was going to live forever? Amenhotep knew that this was a tragedy that should never be repeated. That was why he had taken such pains to establish a succession. In his plan, the princess' father must be firmly established on the throne. North and south must be truly united, so he chose his son-in-law carefully. Thutmoses was a strong, handsome man of war, a great hero, and his wife, Amenhotep's own daughter, adored him. The marriage was popular among the people, and when Pharaoh's own son died, the logical move was to select this young, strong warrior to be his successor. Thutmoses had already fathered a daughter and a son called Amenmoses, so his lineage seemed secure. The decision to elevate Thutmoses to co-regent also set his heart at ease, but this great plan began to crumble when his grandson and oldest granddaughter had died. Hatshepsut's siblings were all gone. And while the little princess in front of him was strong, her mother, his own grown daughter was weak, and would produce no other male heirs. This little princess was the last of his line. His son-in-law, Thutmoses I, was now back from the military campaign that pressed as far as old Babylon. He had arrived to accolades and cheers. The two of them must talk. Perhaps Thutmoses' older boy (Thutmoses II), the son of Mutnofret, his secondary wife, could become the heir. Surely his son-in-law would see the virtue of an arranged marriage between Thutmoses II and Hatshepsut. This would assure the succession by merging the bloodline of the great warrior, with the line of the old kings. That marriage must be in the future.

For now, the two rulers, he and his son-in-law, must be seen together to strengthen their reign. They must also take turns appearing in the capitals of the Upper and Lower Kingdom. He understood how fragile the succession really was, and turned his attention to his granddaughter. The princess was already a good ambassador. The people loved her. *Look at them smile*, he thought. *She loves them too. We must take her North to the Lower Kingdom. Perhaps she will secure the loyalty of the people there as well. They would gladly accept her as queen. The marriage is necessary. The children must see more of each other.*

"Come now, princess. Time to go home."

The young girl climbed back into the chariot and leaned her head on her grandfather's arm. "Yes, Pepi. I am tired. Would you carry me to bed?"

The Great Mother, Ahmose-Nefertari

Back at the palace, Amenhotep carried Hatshepsut to her chamber; her attendants took her lovingly from his arms. He looked in on his bedridden mother; he sat holding her hand for a while, thanking her in his heart for her selfless life. Back in the central chamber he bowed to his wife and made his way to the bedroom of his son-in-law where he stayed well into the night.

9

Chapter 2:
New Orders

In the morning Thutmoses woke just before dawn with his normal military precision. He had a duty to perform and the sooner, the better. He entered the harem complex without being seen by any of the servants and made his way to where his oldest son was sleeping. The boy whose mother called him Twoey (Thutmoses II) sat bolt upright when he realized that it was his father who had waked him. He listened wide-eyed and nodded as his father spoke. He had never done otherwise. He knew his father was a god. His mother reminded him every day. Who would not listen to a god?

Twoey sat still for a long time after his father left. He was confused! In the past his father's orders had always been so sensible. "Walk quietly in the palace grounds. If you hear anyone from the official royal family in the distance turn so as to not meet them. If by accident you do, then lower your eyes, walk slowly past, and never call attention to yourself."

He had found these orders easy to follow. He didn't want to have to speak to anyone, especially the Head Wife and her children. He stayed close to the outer doors of his mother's chambers when he went to the enclosed garden, retreating at the first sound of voices. He planned ahead when he went for archery lessons. He would pass through the main hall of the palace when the others were dining on the veranda. Sometimes he wished he could just spend a day with his father. His mother had made it clear why he could not. He had heard the story often. There had been a time when she was the only wife. Then the old pharaoh had singled out her husband to become the royal husband to the princess who was herself a goddess. Her union with Thutmoses had elevated him to a new level, and all his family was now considered royalty. His mother said she was glad of the marriage and that Twoey was to be grateful for this honor, for it would bring him honor as well.

Twoey's mother often explained that they had privileges above the other harem members because she had been his wife when he was chosen to join the royal family. Before that time they had lived together in a house reserved for military chiefs. Twoey wished they still lived together like that. The new privileges were hard for Twoey to appreciate. He just wanted to spend more time with his father. Food and other provisions were brought to all the harem quarters. Maybe theirs was a little better in quality and quantity than the other families. It was true that when there was a royal procession they did have to follow immediately after the first family. He guessed that made them special. On such occasions Twoey tried hard to keep his father in sight and to march step for step with him. This was hard to do. He sometimes had to take a little skip to adjust his stride which that somehow got out of sync.

The new orders from his father were hard to understand. Had he been dreaming? Did his father really tell him to seek to run into the first family and speak politely to them? What did he mean when he said, "Make friends with the young princess." The princess? He had often seen her. He couldn't think of a thing to say to her. Throughout the day, the boy worried about the new orders. His conclusion was that he would continue his avoidance practices as usual but with one exception, he would hide rather than run away. From a hiding place, he could watch the family and learn more about them. In this way, he would know what to say when the time came. He would speak to the princess as soon as he felt ready.

For the next week he carried out his plan. He had no problem hiding behind a pillar or among the plants in the garden so that he could listen to their conversations. He especially liked to hear the princess talk with her grandfather. More than once he had to suppress a laugh so that he would not get caught in his research. He began to learn about the young girl's habits. She would slip off to the chapel for a few minutes each morning. One day he stood just behind the doorway and watched her talking to the rising sun. He heard her pray that her people would have the food they need to keep them well. He had never made a prayer like that himself. He thought to himself, *She is just a child. No one was making her do that. Where did she get that idea?* More than once he saw her pause in the veranda to pick up a date or honey cake left after a meal. He resolved to carry some dates wrapped in grape leaves so that he could casually offer her one when he finally had the courage to speak to her. She obviously had a sweet tooth. Maybe it would help. How was he to become friends with such a person? He would have to try soon. His father was sure to ask him.

The boy never got a chance to try phase two of his plan. The adults had plans of their own. He would speak to the princess, but it would be his father who would force him to do so.

Chapter 3:
North

It was early in the morning and the old Pharaoh spoke to his granddaughter, "Well my Princess Hatshepsut, would you like to go west over the Nile with me this morning?"

"Is it time for us to die, Pepi? I'm not afraid but I don't want to and I don't want you to either."

"No. It is not time for that," he laughed, shaking his head. "I need to check on the construction of the mortuary temple complex before your Father and I leave to go North to Lower Egypt."

"The place with the big Cat? Can I come? I would like to see the manmade mountains, and I would like to stand between the paws of the great Cat. The great Cat guards the dead pharaohs just like my mau guards me. That's how I *know* that the blood of the pharaohs flows in me."

"Yes, you can come. I would like you to come."

"Can I bring my cat?"

"No, you cannot bring your cat. She might fall off the royal barge looking for her home. Besides, there is a cat that lives on the barge. The barge cat would not welcome your cat. She will be here when you get back. Do you still want to go?"

"Yes, please. But I do wish I could bring my cat."

"Your half-brother will be coming too. Come then. We will take the royal barge to the other side of the Nile. You will see firsthand some workers from Set Ma'at, The Place of Truth."

"Maybe one of them will carve me a cat!"

The young princess ran in front of her grandfather down to the water's edge. She had ridden the barge before but never this direction, never to the *West*, the dwelling place of the dead. "What's the temple complex, Grandfather?"

"The bodies of the dead have to be prepared for the wait for new life. They need a place to be honored."

As the barge approached the building site, Hatshepsut kept looking all around, taking in every feature of the landscape. "Look, Pepi! Look at the mountains. You can see faces in the rocks. Do the spirits hide themselves in the rocks? Are they watching? Pepi! There needs to be a ramp. How can we visit the dead on a chariot without a ramp? They would like to see us chase the sun. Maybe they would laugh if we rode right up to them. The temple complex should have stories on the wall. They would like to read while they are waiting. When I am grown I will have them write our story on the walls here. And I will raise two obelisks, one for you and one for me at the temple on the side of the living that will be so high that the dead will be able to see them and know that you and I honored the gods together. The workers can put stories all over the obelisks as well. I am so glad that you and the Great Mother made the workshops at Set Ma'at."

"Sounds like you have lots of plans for them."

"Lots and lots, Grandfather."

"I will talk to the men, and then we will go and prepare for our trip."

Hatshepsut explored the construction scene while her grandfather consulted with the chief architect, Ineni, about what was to be completed while he was away. When he was finished he signaled the servants and he and Hatshepsut returned to the barge and to the palace complex to make the final preparations for the excursion North.

Hatshepsut informed her grandfather that she had met Senenmut. "How did you find him?" her grandfather asked. "I just looked to see who looked like a relative. I guessed correctly. I told him that I thought we were related. He seemed pleased to be recognized. I asked him to carve me a cat. He said that he would." The Pharaoh resolved to keep a closer eye on his granddaughter.

Egyptian vessels were not constructed like oceangoing vessels. The Nile flowed steadily North and the wind generally blew South. To go North the ships only needed a control drift; to go South a sail could capture the wind and pull the vessel South. Barges were used to convey building materials from quarries to build temples and monuments. Food and other supplies could be conveyed from one part of the nation to another. This barge was a floating diminutive palace. Sleeping quarters and open-air canopies occupied the center part of the vessel. The main control was the large oar in the back that performed the function of a rudder and was used to steer. Oarlocks were set along the side for rowing when more speed was needed. Amenhotep intended to stop at every population center to engage the people. This was going to be a goodwill trip. They would take days to get to the Northern kingdom. He thought it would be an education for the children as well. That afternoon workmen from the craft village carved the names of the two Pharaohs on a rail that would face the Eastern side of the Nile. It was to be a physical reminder to the people of the succession to the throne.

In the morning the royal barge set out following the current downstream. During the first day of the voyage, Hatshepsut sought to make friends with the cat. She dragged her grandfather's royal ceremonial flail behind her until the cat noticed. The second day the cat followed her willingly wherever she went. The workers on the barge began to nudge one another when she came into view. All eyes followed her, laughing at her interaction with the cat. She sat in the shade of the royal canopy to protect herself from the sun, but whenever people were seen on the shore she hurried to the edge of the barge to wave. They in turn always waved back at the diminutive figure with the distinctive *princess lock* which denoted her royal status. The third day the barge workers were negotiating the privilege of waiting on the little princess. There was some sort of morning greeting ceremony that Hatshepsut initiated and executed.

She did not neglect her father and grandfather. She announced to her grandfather that she was glad she left her cat at home because now she had *two* cats. Many games of the board game, Senet, punctuated the travels. Hatshepsut won more than her share. While she played, she plied the men with questions. "Why does Pharaoh carry the flail and crook in most of the carvings?" "Who built the big Pyramids?" Thutmoses, who had spent most of Hatshepsut's childhood away on military campaigns began to see his daughter in a new light. Her older half-brother continued his observations from a distance, unnoticed by Hatshepsut herself.

As the barge headed North the co-regents solidified their friendship and resolve. The romance that they conspired to encourage was on their minds. Thutmose had the beginnings of a plan. He would include military instruction for his son as part of the daily routine. Surely the curious Hatshepsut would be interested. He would encourage his son to speak to the lively Hatshepsut.

Evening was Hatshepsut's favorite time of day. She soon located a spot on the barge where she could sit and watch the sun set in the West. The beauty of the sky resting upon the land of the dead gave her a strange peace. The barge cat usually sat in her lap purring loudly as she stroked its head pushing the ears down to make it look more like a human. She liked thinking about the old Pharaohs. During one such evening she was aware of someone standing behind her. She turned expecting to see her grandfather.

"Oh! You scared me. I thought you were Grandfather."

The boy moved closer and sat down beside her. "No. He and father are talking."

"Isn't the royal barge wonderful? We sit here and watch the country go by. We have all the comforts of the palace. It's a display just for us."

"Father says it is nothing compared to the oceangoing ships of other lands. The barge is good for traveling up and down the Nile where there aren't any storms. Ships that sail on the open sea have more complicated steering mechanisms and more elaborate sails. They are made to sail out of the sight of land and endure storms as strong as our sandstorms."

"What! No! Nothing can be better than Egyptian ships. Don't we have the great mountain tombs that no one else can build? Don't we have the best horses and the fastest chariots? Our ships must be the best."

Her half-brother laughed. "Our land doesn't need oceangoing ships. We trade with the East by sending caravans along the King's Highway. We can go to Palestine, Babylon, and even to the great lands of the East."

"When I am grown up, we will make better ships. We will trade over the ocean. Egypt must be the best."

"I suppose we could study the ships of other nations and make our own oceangoing vessel. We have to go over great mountains to trade with people to the South. If we had great ships we could sail to all those Southern kingdoms. We should be able to do it. I will build great ships with you. We do know how to make things and we do have the best fighters. Our father is a great warrior and his men will follow him anywhere."

"He is handsome. Don't tell Grandfather, but I think father is the *most* handsome man I have ever seen. Mother thinks so, too."

Her half-brother stared ahead and spoke more to himself than Hatshepsut, "He knows all about fighting. He is strong and brave. He doesn't seem to be afraid to go to war. I don't think I can be like him. I don't like to think about killing or fighting for my life. He wants me to learn all the different weapons. He wants me to practice on this trip."

Hatshepsut was quick to respond, "I want to learn. The great Mother fought in the war to unite all Egypt. I am not afraid. I could be like her. I could learn to fight."

"You shouldn't have to fight. There are many soldiers."

"The Pharaohs need to lead their people. I will not be afraid. I do need to learn. Maybe you could teach me what you know."

The conversation continued in a spiraling fashion: boats, war, archery, trade until an attendant came to take the young princess to her bed.

A great sense of relief came over the young prince. They had met. They had spoken. He hadn't even had to use the dates. He would learn more about making boats.

Step Pyramid of King Djoser(Dave Howe)

Chapter 4:
Lessons

The next day, Hatshepsut began her new campaign. After the morning greeting to the servants, she joined her father and grandfather who were having their morning meal of bread and dried fruit.

The young girl leaned forward, "Tell me again. Why do all the pictures of Pharaoh and Osiris show them holding the flail and the crook?"

Her grandfather who was used to the perpetual flow of questions answered first. "The Pharaoh rules to serve others not to be served by them. The flail, as you know, is one stick chained to several sticks. It was not designed to tame cats though you seem to have been able to use it for that purpose. It is used beat stalks of grain. One blow of a stick is multiplied into three. The grain is loosened from the stalk, and then the chaff can be blown away by the wind. Pharaoh carries this to remind himself and the people of his duty to provide for the feeding of his people. The great Imhotep saved the people by wisely stockpiling grain for the years of drought. Pharaohs have created storehouses of grain ever since. One of our purposes in this journey North is to initiate the building of new storehouses.

"The crook is the sign of a shepherd. Kings are really shepherds. They lead the people. The curved part of the crook is used to gently turn an animal that is going the wrong way. It has saved the life of many a young calf or sheep. The crook can be used to fend off wild animals as well. The king is to lead his people gently like a shepherd. He should see the direction of the nation and be a good shepherd to his people."

Thutmoses took up the tale. "Both tools have proved to be formidable weapons of war. Many an enemy has fled when faced with the wildly flailing sticks. The flail can kill a man if used correctly. The crook is a good defensive weapon. It can deflect the blows of others, and it can be used as a bludgeon itself. Of course, I would never go to war without good archers who can attack from a distance or the brave axe men who fight so fiercely."

During the middle of this explanation the boy Thutmoses joined the breakfast party. After her father's explanation Hatshepsut announced that she and her brother were ready to learn to use the weapons of war. Thutmoses said that his son was already becoming a skilled archer with the beginning bow. He may have been exaggerating to impress the young princess. Hatshepsut looked at her half-brother with a quizzical look. "Well, I better catch up then. When do we begin?"

Thutmoses agreed to lessons in the early morning before the sun got too hot. "We will begin with the crook. Here is one that has been cut down to match your size. We will begin with learning how to use the staff to block a blow." Throughout the voyage the lessons went well. Hatshepsut was not afraid to try anything, and when she whirled the flail around her head, Thutmoses began to think she could be a warrior after all. The children began to greet each other before the lessons and the two kings were content.

Every evening the two children met to watch the sunset. The young prince automatically handed the princess a date. Sometimes they would sit quietly. At other times they spoke of the lessons they were practicing. Most often their conversation turned to the making of boats. When they returned home, they would begin making toy models. Then they would get the craftsmen to help build the real thing.

Hatshepsut: The Pharaoh's Daughter

At the major population centers the royal foursome met with the sub rulers, the viziers and noble families. Sometimes they hosted meals on the barge. At every encounter Hatshepsut charmed the people. She smiled, nodded, and bowed. She asked questions of everyone and listened carefully to the replies. She won the hearts of the people everywhere. In the years to come they often spoke to one another of the visit of the young Pharaoh's daughter and her pleasing manners.

As the party traveled North, Amenhotep told the children something of the primary deity of each region. Bat was already known to them as was the cow-goddess at their home. They passed through the land of Anubis. As they approached the Northern Kingdom, he told them about the honor given to the sacred bull Apis. He told how the bulls were mummified like the Pharaohs themselves.

He told them that the area was the capitol of Hatshepsut's favorite Pharaoh Pepi. They would see Pepi's small tomb that was not too far from the famous step pyramid of King Djoser. Imhotep, a famous servant of the king, was the architect of that first great stone pyramid. When they arrived at the pyramid, the children took great interest in the construction of all the buildings and the tombs.

They wanted to know more about Imhotep.

Hatshepsut asked, Where did he come from?"

Her grandfather told her, "It was a long time ago. King Djoser had some very disturbing dreams. None of the priests could tell him their meaning. One of the palace servants remembered a prisoner from another land who had correctly interpreted a dream that he had been given years earlier. Djoser sent for him and he was able to interpret the pharaoh's dream. When Djoser asked what his name was, he answered in his own language. It sounded like he said something like Hotep which means *came in peace* in Egyptian. They began to call him Imhotep which means *he who came in peace.* It seemed like a good name. He not only came in peace; he helped maintain peace in the land for a long time.

"We better be getting back to the barge. Tomorrow we will see the Great Pyramid. Look, you can see them there." Their grandfather pointed out the Giza pyramids, their smooth sides reflecting the sunlight, far off near the horizon.

The Great Cat (Elisabeth Howe)

Chapter 5:
Giza

Hatshepsut hardly slept. She did her best to hurry the morning meal. Finally the moment came and Hatshepsut saw for herself the great manmade mountains on the Giza plateau. She stood, taking in the shining sight, and the contrasting shadows that the three great pyramids played out.

Her grandfather stood beside her. He signaled to the father and son, who were both called Thutmoses, to come closer and he began. "Look at the pyramids and the shadows. Our scholars have begun to read the old records from the real Pepi's time. Those who understand the mathematics can read the seasons from those shadows. We need to be able to read the signs so we can tell when to expect the flooding of the Nile and know when to harvest and when to plant. We think that Pepi's scholars also knew the size of the earth and that the royal cubit is related to it. They kept their secrets so that Egypt would have advantage over the other nations. It is just as important for you children to restore and learn that knowledge, as it is to learn to use the tools of war. We will gather all the manuscripts and have them copied at Set Ma'at. It will be part of your schooling. You will have to learn more of their mathematics if you are determined to raise those obelisks. The secrets used to build the pyramids themselves have made us the greatest civilization of the world. Did you know that the *smallest* stones inside that pyramid weigh as much as twenty men! The smallest stones! The largest stones weigh as much as 700 men! Only we Egyptians know the secret of how to build with such stones."

"The pharaohs are buried there, aren't they, Pepi?" interrupted Hatshepsut.

"Yes they are. They are the pharaohs of Egypt's greatest age. There are secret chambers in those pyramids. There are secret doors and, some say, secret tunnels under the pyramids. There is a chamber with a boat for the use of the dead. Rumor has it that if the secret door were opened, the light from the North Star would shine into the pharaoh's tomb. No one can find the secret door. The stones are so finely cut, and the door is on a hidden hinge. The mass of the stones themselves and the carefully designed venting passages keep the inside tombs at a constant, cool temperature. Even on the hottest day of the year, or during a sandstorm, the temperature doesn't change!"

Hatshepsut again interrupted, but in a distracted manner. She was talking to herself, "The East is for the living; the West is for the dead..." Her voice trailed off; a puzzled look passed over her face then she found her voice once again. "The big Cat! I see it. Help me! Help me! I want to stand between its paws. Look Pepi. It faces the East. It does guard the sleeping pharaohs. I knew it would!" The child began to run toward the colossal structure. The adults followed at a slower pace. Thutmoses II took up the rear. He wondered how his younger half-sister knew so much more than he did about their history.

Hatshepsut stood between the paws of the colossal structure with her hands on her hips, staring. She turned toward them and shouted, "There's an obelisk between his paws. There's an obelisk between his paws! Why is there an obelisk between his paws?"

Her grandfather answered. "Clear away the sand. You will see marks on the stone. The shadow of the obelisk can be used to mark the seasons of the year as well as the hour of the day. Even I can read these marks. It was these marks that made me look for the old papyri. I found secrets lost for a thousand years! All because old Pepi didn't make sure who was going to rule when he was gone." He gave a quick look and small nod to his son-in-law with the comment.

Hatshepsut moved toward the obelisk. She pressed her back against the stone and looked East. She raised her arms and stood still for a while. "That's what I want to do. It's our job to help them. The old pharaohs need to be protected from the living while they wait for new life. The great cat was put here to protect them. We will have to protect those who are buried near our home."

The party made its way back to the barge. Hatshepsut kept up her usual commentary. "I didn't know that the great cat was painted. He wears the Pharaoh's headdress. I wonder why it is crowned with the cobra? It is a *big* cat. I will have to tell mother."

Semitic People depicted on a mural. Notice the beards and hair.

Chapter 6:

Slaves

When they arrived back at the royal barge, the servants had fresh squeezed juice waiting for them. The barge was untied and they continued on the journey North. The children ran up and down waving to the crowd that was gathering. The adults also waved but didn't join the frantic races of the children. Thutmoses looked at the crowd along the shore, "Who are these people? They certainly are not Egyptians. Look at the beards. I fought people who looked a lot like them during my last major military campaign past the Sinai. They were fierce opponents."

His father-in-law answered him, "These people are called the Hebrews after Eber, one of their forefathers. They have been in Egypt for hundreds of years. They first came here long ago by invitation of pharaoh himself. One of their number, the great Imhotep whose work we saw yesterday, had saved all Egypt. Pharaoh Djoser was so grateful he gave the best land in all Egypt for them to live in. Everything grows well here. Pharaoh had been warned in a dream about a famine that was going to come in seven years. The dream had troubled him, but he didn't know what it meant. Imhotep understood the dream and advised Pharaoh to set aside food during days of plenty so that the nation was prepared for the seven-year famine that followed. Pharaoh trusted him more than anyone in the country, and he was made the supervisor all of the king's projects. When the famine came, all of the neighboring nations became dependent upon us and much of their wealth was given in exchange for food. Imhotep actually used the famine to unite all of Egypt. We have had to fight to unite upper and lower Egypt. He managed it without a single battle. He bought Upper Egypt by trading property deeds for food. In the end he was able to concentrate on building and learning rather than war. Some say that he invented the making of papyri and the keeping of records. His medical handbook has been found and is being copied at Set Ma'at. We owe him a lot. Of course, after the death of Pepi all that history was forgotten. The new rulers took back the rich land and forced the Hebrews to work as slaves. They did not fight back when that happened. They are working now at restoring the buildings of the Old Kingdom."

"Nonetheless, they are not Egyptians. It looks like there are more of them in this area than true Egyptians. What will happen if our enemies invade? They may turn on us and join them. We've got to control their numbers. So many children die when they are young. Maybe we can arrange to make sure that their boy babies are among them."

The old man shuddered. He hated the thought of deliberately killing any children. He hated judging a people by their appearance. His mother's skin was dark; his father's light. He never dismissed servants or workers based on appearance. Yet, he and his son-in-law needed to work together.

"You will have to make the arrangements. I will support you in this. We must do everything to keep the nation safe. Have you begun to talk to the boy about his duties if he becomes Pharaoh?"

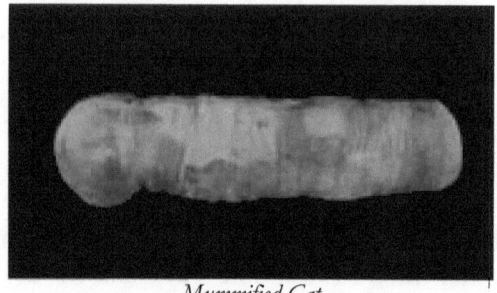

Mummified Cat

Chapter 7:
Bast

As the barge made its way to the Nile Delta, the oarsman directed the royal barge into a channel on the right, moved it parallel to the shore, and moored it there. At the evening meal the old Pharaoh spoke to Hatshepsut. "I have a surprise for you, princess. Tomorrow we will visit the ruins of an old temple made by Pepi himself. Guess what god they honored there?"

Hatshepsut furrowed her brow. "Not bulls again?"

"No. Something you like better. I think it will be your favorite."

Hatshepsut again furrowed her brow. She lifted up her eyes to the sky. Then she broke into a laugh. "Cats! Is it cats, Pepi?"

"I knew you would guess. Yes, this region of Egypt considers the cat their great protector. The people of this region often kept cats for pets because of the number of snakes along the many branches of the Nile. Some of the snakes are poisonous. The cats were able to keep them out of the houses. The story goes that there was a time when a plague struck Egypt and many people died, but the areas with the cats never contracted the disease. After that, cats were honored and the bodies of many cats were mummified and buried like the pharaohs themselves. The temple is called the temple of Bast."

"Pepi! Now I see. No wonder the Big Cat is wearing the cobra on his crown. He is the king of the snakes and can protect the Pharaohs from all those terrors as well. I do want to see the ruins. We need more cats in all of Egypt if they protect us from disease. I thought they were just friends."

"I am planning to take you to my favorite spot in all of Egypt. It is near the ruins of the temple. We will have to take many servants with us though. My father took me there when I was about your age. It was one of the happiest times of my life."

"Will my brother come with us?"

"No. It will be just you and me and the servants. Thutmoses will spend some of the time practicing archery while we are gone. I don't want you to try your hand at archery on the ship. Anyway, you are too small. You will have to be much stronger to pull back on the bow. Your father is the best archer I have ever seen. It takes all his strength. I have seen many an arrow go astray because the archer could not control the bow. It's just too dangerous. We will have more fun; you will see. Besides I think your father has some other business and will take your brother with him."

The two made their way to the temple ruins. Around thirty servants followed behind. As they walked, the old man pointed out that the river was calm. "Do you know why it is so still?"

"No, Pepi. I did wonder."

"This is a wadi, not the river itself. A wadi is a river bed that doesn't always make its way to the sea. During the flood season this water will rise and run fiercely toward the ocean. Now it is just an inlet with calm water."

The couple found the foundations of the temple and discovered a few of the buried cat mummies. Hatshepsut asked about the wrappings and the masks. They found a place to sit where they could imagine the temple before it fell into ruins. Hatshepsut insisted that her grandfather tell her the story about how the cats once saved the people of the area. After a while the servants brought them a light meal, and they sat looking out at the water while they ate. Amenhotep asked Hatshepsut if she guessed why they had brought the servants.

"Did they come to guard us?"

"You could say so. They will guard us from crocodiles. You will see."

He led her to a place where the wadi split again into two branches. He ordered the servants to line the bank on each side.

"What are they trying to do, Grandfather? They're just standing there!"

"We will wait a little while. If there are any crocodiles near, they will smell the humans and be afraid. They will leave the area and we will be safe. The servants will continue to stand watch and if one happens to stay, the servants will jump into the water and hold its mouth shut until we get safely away. For now we are going in the water. You and I are going to swim. I will show you the games my father taught me."

All afternoon grandfather and granddaughter played. They floated on their backs. They raced from one bank to the other. Sometimes Hatshepsut won. The servants were never quite sure that the old man didn't cheat. They explored the plants that grew along the bank and gathered baskets full of lotus flowers that they handed to the servants. They happened upon the nest of a heron, and Hatshepsut wondered at the life that was contained inside the eggs. The Heron herself gave a cry to distract the observers and flew past them, swooping over the water. The blue-gray of the feathers caused Hatshepsut to stare in wonder. The soaring of the great bird over her head made her catch her breath for a moment. She thought she had never seen anything so majestic. "We better leave his egg alone. I want them to live here." They moved carefully and silently away from the nest.

When they were clear of the close rushes her grandfather said, "Let me teach you to play crocodile, princess."

"What! Is there a crocodile?"

"No. Don't be afraid. Stand still here with your legs apart. You will ride the crocodile."

The curious Hatshepsut did as she was told. Her grandfather stood behind her. She heard movement in the water as he walked away. The servants on the shore began to smile. Some began to laugh, recalling their own childhood memories. Soon her grandfather swam between her legs and raised her up out of the water. He managed to say, "Hold on." Hatshepsut balanced herself on her grandfather-crocodile. The old man swam round and round carrying the laughing child. When he finally stood up, Hatshepsut slid off his back. "Oh, Grandfather! Let's do that again!"

"In a moment, child, I'm not as young as I used to be. Let me catch my breath. Your mother loved that game as well. It was easier then!"

"Did you bring her here, too?"

"Just one time. I don't know if she remembers. She was a little younger than you."

Though he was weary, the crocodile ride was repeated several times. Finally the old man said, "We better dry off and go back."

As they made their way back to the barge, Hatshepsut volunteered, "I don't know which I like better, chasing the sun or riding the crocodile. I used to think that there could be nothing more fun than chasing the sun."

" You can like them both."

"I love you, Pepi."

Chapter 8:
Serious Orders

While the old pharaoh and Hatshepsut explored the river, Thutmoses, with his son by his side, made enquiries and found that two Egyptian midwives who delivered the Hebrew children were Puah and Shiphrah. Thutmoses ordered them to appear before him on the royal barge. He began by appealing to their love of Egypt. He told them that the safety of the country was depending on them. Their help was needed. The women indicated that they would be glad to do what they could for Egypt. The pharaoh then told them that they were to neglect the boy babies of the Hebrew slaves when they were born. They might forget to clear their air passages. They might squeeze the small bodies to stop the breathing. They could let the girl babies live because they would not grow up to be such a threat. The women bowed, understanding their orders, but appalled by them.

As they made their way back home from the barge, the women discussed what they should do. They agreed that they must not kill the children. They had become midwives because they never tired of hearing that first breath of the spirit. That first cry was music to their ears. In the end they came up with a plan. They would continue with their work as usual. If they were called in for questioning, they would declare that the Hebrew women were so strong that the babies were born before the midwives came on the scene. They could avoid condemnation and still let the babies live. It would be risky but what else could they do? They would not kill children even for Egypt.

Chapter 9:
Dinner

That evening at dinner, the two kings talked of the duties of the pharaohs and their obligations to the people. For the benefit of the children, they explained, once again, how Egypt had often been divided into Upper and Lower Egypt and that they had a plan to keep it united. They wanted the children to help. They planned to visit all the important families in Lower Egypt. The children needed to be on their best behavior and greet the people. Hatshepsut objected saying that she was always on her best behavior with the people. "That is why they love me." The two kings exchanged knowing glances.

Thutmoses continued, "You children and I are going to take the barge home and Hatshepsut's grandfather will stay here for two or three cycles of the Nile. We feel that both Upper and Lower Egypt need to know the presence of a pharaoh. The nation has been divided so many times that we need to maintain a palace in the North and the South. It will be good for Egypt. The people will develop loyalty to the royal family.

"I will have a lot to do when we return home. I am planning a military campaign to the South. It will be easier to work with soldiers in the Southern Kingdom. When the time comes for me to go out to battle, Amenhotep will return to the palace in the South."

Hatshepsut turned to her grandfather, "You're not coming with us, Pepi?"

"No. Like your father said, I need to do this for Egypt. I have to stay here for now. The time will pass quickly. We all have a lot to do. You will have a great trip home. They will have to use the sails. I will not stay away too long. I want to be near my mother when her time comes."

Hatshepsut turned to her brother, "We will learn how the sails work." The two children nodded to each other, knowingly. The pharaohs exchanged a quizzical look. "What was that all about?" it seemed to say.

Chapter 10:
Home Again

The children loved the trip home. Hatshepsut missed her grandfather, but enjoyed the time with her father. He continued to teach both of them the use of the staff and flail. For the first time in his life he began to see his children as people who had ideas of their own. The two children never stopped thinking about their boat project. They paid special attention to any change in the sails, plying the servants with questions. They would sit and watch the wind pull the barge against the current. In the evening they watched the sunset and argued about the layout of the ship they would build when they were grown. Thutmoses did remember to bring out his stash of dates during their evening talks. He even reminded Hatshepsut that she needed to be sure and clean her teeth with a brushing stick when she ate dates. "My mother says that if I don't do that a worm will come and eat into my teeth and it might even eat into my head! Ugh! You don't want that to happen."

Hatshepsut shrugged and said, "I am careful to lick all the sweetness off my teeth. Don't worry about me."

When they arrived at the palace, Hatshepsut bombarded her mother with questions. "Do you remember the crocodile game? Did grandfather take you to see old Pepi's ruins and the Big Cat? Did you find any cat mummies when you were there?" Hatshepsut enjoyed listening to every detail about her mother's childhood.

After she described a gold mask she had seen as a child she said, "Oh! That reminds me. There's a present for you. It's from Senenmut, your cousin. He said you requested it. I promised to give it to you myself."

"It's my cat! I know it's my cat!" Her mother produced the cat statue from behind a screen. "Oh, Mother! It is so beautiful. It looks like a real cat. Can we go tomorrow and thank him?"

"Your father and I will take you to his house so you can thank him."

"Where is my palace cat? I haven't seen her." The princess left her mother and was heard calling "Meow. Meow. Meow," throughout the palace. After a prolonged interval the cat appeared, but turned her back on Hatshepsut and turned away when Hatshepsut tried to pet her. But in the morning all was forgiven and the cat took up her watchful care of the young princess.

In the late afternoon Pharaoh ordered a chariot and a driver to take the royal family to the crossing place near the craft city. A small papyrus boat carried them to the other side of the Nile, where, once again, a chariot took them to Dier el Medina, the Place of Truth, Set Ma'at. They made their way to the house of Senenmut. Pharaoh left his wife and daughter to visit with him and thank him for her cat while he sought out the senior Ineni to discuss his own building projects that would be carried out during the next dry season. Little did he know that his daughter began to fill Senenmut's mind with plans for her own future projects including the boat project. On the way home Hatshepsut began to carry out some experiments on the boat. She would shift her weight and take note of the changes in the motion of the light boat. She was glad she that Senenmut had promised to help with the project.

In the days to come Thutmoses, his wife, and Hatshepsut began to take an evening ride along the route that Amenhotep had used. Hatshepsut said they didn't know how to chase the sun but she did enjoy standing between her parents with both arms behind them just the same. The people enjoyed it as well. The crowds increased in size and the trio continued the tradition of stopping to greet the people on the way home. Thutmoses began to see that his father-in-law was even wiser than he thought. He could see the growing affection that the people had for his family. He would be sure to talk again about the things he could do to encourage loyalty the next time they were together. Once in a while his Twoey would join them, and four figures crowded into the sun-chasing chariot. Thutmoses was glad to see that Hatshepsut did not seem to mind. He was careful to avoid alarming her by having his son come every evening.

The campaign into Nubia was ahead. His last campaign to the East had been successful. One good push to the South, requiring tribute from neighboring kingdoms, should secure the peace for many years. The eastern trade routes took Egyptian ropes, pottery, and glass to far away nations. The granaries were full. Scholarship was on the increase. The temple complex was being expanded on the East and Amenhotep's funerary temple was nearly finished on the West. Thutmoses finished planning his Southern campaign and waited for conditions to be favorable for the trip up the Nile. He would make several appearances in the Northern capitol with his father-in-law. He would check on the effectiveness of his orders to the midwives and the two kings would return South. Amenhotep would have time with his mother, daughter, and granddaughter while the Southern border was secured.

The day finally came. Hatshepsut begged to go with her father. He said the trip was going to be a quick one. He would take a smaller vessel. The Nile was in a new cycle of inundation and the current was swift. Some of the trip would be made by chariot, and when they were on the water, the rowers would be used. As soon as the Nile could be navigated against the annual inundation, they would return. Once the new crops were planted the Southern campaign could begin. When the campaign was over the two leaders would reverse locations. The younger Pharaoh and his family would move North, and the older Pharaoh would remain in the South. "You know your grandfather has no greater wish than that everything be done to establish the dynasty. He believes this trading palaces is good for the people."

Reluctantly and with understanding beyond her years, the princess sighed and said, "I know. At least when you go to Nubia, Pepi and I can be together."

Chapter 11:
More Orders

When Thutmoses arrived at the Northern Capital, the two pharaohs hosted a banquet for the oldest families. This time they didn't have the princess with them to facilitate their efforts. The next day Thutmoses was eager to tour the delta area to see how effective the policy had worked out with the midwives.

As they moved through the village, they saw many toddlers near the homes of the slaves. "What is this?" He turned to the chief officer. "Bring me the midwives," he said pausing to recall, "their names are Puah and Shiphrah."

When the women arrived the king spoke sternly, "Why do I see so many young boys among the Hebrew people?"

"My lord, the Hebrew women are not like the Egyptian women for they are lively and deliver before we arrive. They are nursing the child by the time we get there. We don't have the chance to do as you suggested."

The Pharaoh's face grew red and his body shook, but he said nothing in reply. After a pause he dismissed them and spoke more to himself. "We have to make a law."

The next day when the court was assembled, the pharaohs signed into law an edict that stated that every newborn Hebrew boy was to be cast into the Nile. Severe penalties were to be leveled against any family or midwife that refused. The older pharaoh shuddered as he placed his seal on the document. This securing the kingdom had a price he hadn't considered. He secretly hoped that Thutmoses would soon relent and not see the young children as a threat. He suggested that the royal craftsmen, who were in the area, conduct workshops among the slaves to see if any young children could be taught to carve the temple hieroglyphics on plaster walls. The most talented could be sent to Set Ma'at to become master craftsmen. "If we separate the children from their people, they will not rise up against us." Thutmoses agreed that it would be a good idea for the boys that were already growing up, but he did not show any hesitation about the new law.

In the end it was Amenhotep who visited the craftsmen and described the vision of Set Ma'at and how he wanted them to gather more of the records of the Old Kingdom, identify those who could become gifted craftsmen. "Start a school for the young. Include the slaves. Teach those who learn quickly how to read. Teach them to write the symbols as well. Teach them the plaster methods that allow us to write on the walls of our holy places. Identify those who are gifted with carving and metal work. With your help we will restore the glory of the Old Kingdom."

Every day the navigator checked the winds to see if the time were right for the trip South. When the time came, the craft school was established. Amenhotep had spent a good deal of time with the children, marveling at the speed at which some learned the symbols and the plaster crafts.

Hatshepsut, the princess: (Dave Howe)

Chapter 12:
Pepi

Many days later the young princess kept watch from the entrance of the palace. "I see it. They're coming!" She ran through the palace spreading the good news. The servants smiled as she passed. They looked forward to seeing the old familiar sight of the chasing of the sun. When the barge finally landed, Hatshepsut had already jumped on board. She rushed to her grandfather. She closed her eyes and hugged him with all her might. When she finally let go, he looked down at her. "My, princess, you have grown. You look like a young woman now."

"Yes Pepi, look at my grownup's clothes." As she spun around in front of him the light cloth surrounded her with a halo of motion. He smiled with approval. His granddaughter was eager to speak, "I still remember how to chase the sun. Mother and Father go with me, but they have never learned to tell me the stories like you."

He took her hand and together they laughingly recited, "The East is for the living. The West is for the dead. The Nile will bring new life!"

"I'm so glad you're back, Pepi."

"I've missed being called that," he answered.

"Can we chase the sun tonight?"

"I thought perhaps that you would have outgrown that game."

"I will never outgrow chasing the sun."

"I am very tired. I think it will have to wait until tomorrow."

"You will tell me a story though, won't you?"

"Yes, princess."

Amenhotep went to see his mother. Much to his surprise she was a bit improved. She recognized him and he sat with her as she ate her simple dinner.

During the formal welcome home dinner Hatshepsut insisted on sitting between her father and grandfather. The servants watched with approval. She plied her grandfather with questions. He told her about the renovations of the old temples. "Even the one for the cats?" she asked.

"Yes, even the one for the cats. In fact I have had a small compound built near my favorite spot so that we don't have to stay on the barge when we go there. It's like a miniature palace. I have had the craftsmen make some surprises for you."

"When, Pepi? When can we go?"

"I don't know my child. We will know when the time is right. No promises for now."

"Too much fun, Pepi! Oh! I forgot. Let me show you the cat Senenmut made me." She ran to her quarters and returned with the exquisite cat.

"Did Senenmut make this himself?"

"Yes. We visit the craft village almost every week. I tell him all my ideas. He seems to understand exactly what I want to build when I am grown."

"Oh, princess. I was wrong. You have not changed much. You have as many ideas as ever."

"More, Pepi, more! Thutmoses, my brother, and I are going to build a great ship when we are grown. We will sail it on the big water and trade that way. We will go farther than any Egyptians before us."

The old man laughed. "I can't wait to see that, princess. I believe that you will do it." He risked a nod of approval to his son-in-law. He had been working on their goal.

The conversation turned to the studies of the children. This prompted the pharaoh telling them about the new craft school in the North. He could not hide his pleasure in the new idea. "I believe that the best of the students should come here to learn the metal crafts as well as the plaster crafts that they will study there. I have been telling your father that if we educate the slaves in the great crafts, they will come to love Egypt as we do. They will want to help us restore it to the glory of the time past."

The young people went off to bed. Amenhotep congratulated Thutmoses on the friendship between the two children. "Good idea that ship building."

"I had nothing to do with it. It was all Hatshepsut's idea. She is preoccupied with it. You should see the pictures they draw and the models they make."

The older man excused himself, "I am tired," he said. On his way to his own chamber he stopped again to look in on his bedridden mother. Once again he thanked her for the idea of the craft village. He stopped at Hatshepsut's door and looked in on the sleeping princess. She stirred. In a soft voice he said, "See you in the morning, princess." He thought she opened her eyes for a moment, but she soon turned and fell back asleep. Contented and thankful, he made his way to his own bed.

Chapter 13:

Mourning

The palace woke early. Servants consulted with one another and finally the chief steward made his way to the rooms of the younger king. Thutmoses went to the reception room where he sat still for a long time. When the sun came up, he returned to his rooms and woke his wife. He left her in the care of her attendants and returned to the empty reception room.

He then went to wake Hatshepsut, but an old and trusted servant woman who had never spoken to him before said, "My king, let her sleep. Who knows when she will sleep well again!"

"Very well, let me know the very moment you hear any sound from her room."

Thoughts came fast and furiously to his mind. *How could it be? He wasn't ready. The plans were working. The old man was so wise. Yesterday he looked so strong. Who would have guessed that he would go before his mother? The children, the children are not ready. My wife is overcome with grief. This is worse than war. There is no one to fight. Who knows when it will end?*

He gave the order for the chief servants to come to him. "I will need all your help. I know you love the Great Mother, my wife, and the young princess. I do not think we should tell the Mother. It would kill her. She is used to her son being gone. We will let her have peace. The body will not be ready for burial for some time. She need not know." The servants nodded in approval. "I do not know how I can help the princess. Amenhotep was the joy of her life. May the gods give me wisdom. Perhaps I could declare Amenhotep to be enthroned the patron god of Set Ma'at, his favorite work. The princess would like that idea. I am sure he will watch over that village forever, don't you?"

Just then a servant came to say that Hatshepsut was moving around in her chamber. Thutmoses made his way and knocked softly on the door. The princess opened the door. "Pepi, today we chase the sun! Oh, father, I thought you were Pepi."

"May I come in?" Thutmoses sat in a chair near the princess' couch. "Sit down." The princess sat down on the corner edge of her couch. All was quiet for a long time. Finally her father spoke. "Pepi has travelled to the West."

"Why didn't someone wake me? I would have wanted to go with him."

"He has made the journey that we must each take alone."

For a moment the princess looked puzzled. Soon her quick mind drew the inevitable conclusion. "No! It cannot be. I just saw him at my door. He spoke to me. I remember seeing him." He said, "See you in the morning, princess. I heard him!"

"That was last night. He stopped to look in on you on his way to bed. The servant who made the rounds at the 4th hour noticed that he was not breathing. You were the last person he saw. He is gone now. The servants carried his body to the funerary temple that was just completed. His will be the first body to be cared for there. I have told the servants not to tell your great-grandmother. She will join him soon enough. He is now the patron god of Set Ma'at. He will inspire craftsmanship and creativity for years to come."

Hatshepsut sat very still, more still than she had ever sat before. Her father thought she aged before his eyes. The lightheartedness faded and the tears came. She clung to her father and she sobbed. Exhausted she laid down again on her bed. Thutmoses signaled to her favorite attendant, the one who had requested that she be allowed to sleep. The woman leaned over the girl and stroked her back as she spoke softly to her. Thutmoses retreated once again.

Hatshepsut stayed in her room for quite some time. Gradually her mind cleared. She made her way to where her father was seated. "The people," she said. "How will you tell the people?"

"We will have to send couriers throughout the whole land. We must begin today. If we send the right message the people will not be afraid. They know that I am Pharaoh and they are used to me, a little. When your grandfather made me co-regent, I thought him hasty. I see now that he was right. The people do not need uncertainty. When they don't who is to rule, they do not know how to carry on. I will have to give the people that certainty as well. I will have to announce the next pharaoh even if it is too soon for a co-regency. You are the one with the royal blood. Your grandfather was preparing you. How many times did he say, 'You are the daughter of the pharaoh. You will be the wife of the pharaoh, the sister of the pharaoh and the mother of the pharaoh. I think we will have to announce your engagement to the next pharaoh."

Thutmoses couldn't believe that he was talking so frankly with his young daughter, but it was clear to him that she was the only one who would understand what he meant. "It will have to be soon."

"Can't I be pharaoh? I can fight. I am strong. When I am grown, I will be even stronger. I will work every day to get stronger."

"You will have to be the mother of pharaoh. You must marry. Shall we also announce that you are betrothed to Thutmoses, my oldest son?"

The girl looked dazed. "What!"

"You will make him pharaoh, just as your royal mother made me Pharaoh. So it has been for several generations. You will reign together."

"I cannot think about that. I just want to be alone for a while. I miss Pepi so. I always talked to him about everything. If I go to all our favorite places, maybe I will know what he would want."

"You know what he would want."

"I do not feel it. Can I take a chariot out tonight and pretend I am with Pepi? I will take the gentlest horses. Can I then take my best servants and some of the soldiers and go to where grandfather and I spent those last happy days. Perhaps my heart will settle and I can answer. Pepi will help me find peace. Perhaps I can bring some of the new workers back here to Set Ma'at like he said. I will be carrying out his wish."

Her father sat and thought. He spoke, thinking out loud. "Perhaps it would be best. The people will understand your pilgrimage; they know how much you loved him. It will give them something to think about. We can send couriers with the barge to make announcements in the cities. Do not stay too long. You should return by the time his body is ready. We will plan a great celebration of his enthronement as a god. The ceremonies will help the people with their grief and unify them just as he would wish. I will make the arrangements; you can leave on the third day. In the meantime help me with your great-grandmother and your mother. I will direct the barge's navigator to take you to that small palace your grandfather mentioned. It seems he was building it for you. I will move quickly on this."

Thutmoses was glad for the work. Finally he had something to do. He had a direction. Giving orders calmed his mind and strengthened his resolve to do his duty. He would put his most trusted officer in charge of the princess' safety. After the funeral he would still have to go on the Nubian campaign. He must make a show of strength. Hatshepsut would be his confidant. She seemed able to understand his burden. His son would need her strength. He could not be pharaoh without her.

That evening Hatshepsut took out a chariot alone. The crowds still assembled. She did not chase the sun at any great speed, but she held out her arm to her grandfather and spoke to him just the same. There was not a dry eye among the people as she passed.

She stopped the chariot and looked toward the West. She called out, "Pepi, do you see me? I will build a monument to you. I will learn how to raise the two obelisks to remember our love just as I promised. I will be strong. I am going North. Come with me."

During the drive back she drove the chariot even more slowly, but she still stopped at the usual places. Each time the people suppressed their tears and bowed to the young princess. As she drove away mingled phrases could be heard, "So brave. So grown up. So strong. So beautiful."

Thutmoses watched her return from the palace steps and marveled at the composure of his daughter. "The blood of the gods does flow in her veins. Egypt needs her." His son would need her. His son needed more training in everything. The king saw that clearly. His son was shy, not very strong physically or mentally. He hardly spoke his mind. True, he was compliant, perhaps too compliant. He attempted to do all that was asked of him but needed constant validation. If only he had a tenth of Hatshepsut's initiative. He must one day be able to go out on a military campaign of his own. He must join in the regular training of the guard. He will become stronger. He must have a victory to give him more courage. The father decided that when he went on the Southern campaign, he would leave a small pocket of resistance and send his son out to finish the job and return to the accolades of the people.

In the evening Thutmoses saw his daughter enter the chamber of her great-grandmother. He moved closer to the door so that he could overhear the conversation. "Great Mother, I am going to take a trip. Pepi wants me to visit the craftsmen in the North and bring the best students back to your city. You know I visit it every day. I showed you the cat that Senenmut made me. Isn't it wonderful that you made a school where such skill can be taught? Can I keep Senenmut's cat in your room until I get back? Don't worry about me. Pepi will watch over me." The old woman smiled, reminded of her favorite accomplishment, a school to restore the glory of Egypt. "Bless you my child."

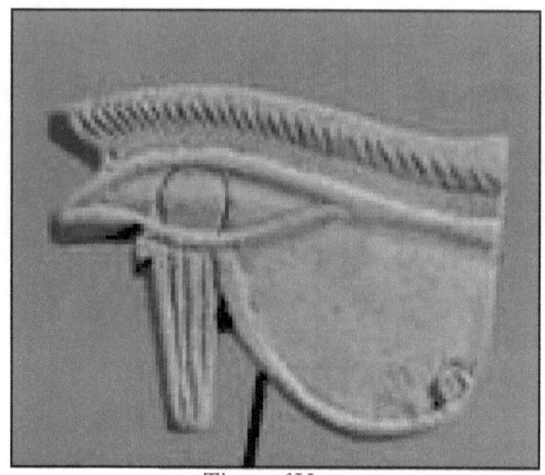
The eye of Horus

Chapter 14:
Orders to the Captain

Hatshepsut retired to her room and Thutmoses sent for his most faithful warrior captain, Ramose, himself a prince of Egypt. Around his neck he wore the sign of Wedjat, the eye of Horus. The amulet was descriptive. The man seemed to have eyes in the back of his head. He had driven the pharaoh's chariot in many a battle. They had made a good team. Ramose could maneuver skillfully through a crowd, driving steadily enough for Thutmoses to use his bow to advantage. More than once the skill of the driver had saved both lives. Thutmoses always liked having him at his back during a battle. He wanted his ever-watchful eye keeping his Hatshepsut safe.

When the soldier arrived Thutmoses began, "My friend, I know I promised you some time to spend with your family. Is your wife well?"

"Yes. She delivered the child last week. They are both well."

"You have other children as well?"

"Yes. My first wife was lost to me along with her child. I thought I would never know joy again. Then I met and married Isis. The gods have been good to us. She is so strong. We now have five sons. Two of them are already learning the military arts. This last boy seems to be the strongest yet. You should have heard him when he was born. It sounded like he was ready to take on any challenge. He is gaining weight and growing every day."

"I know your first sorrow. You know we lost our two oldest children. Hatshepsut is now the only child of the Amosis line. She alone of my children carries the blood of the old Pharaohs. She must be kept safe. She will have to marry the next ruler of Egypt, or the whole land may fall into disarray. Our enemies will be able to take advantage of any lapse of leadership. Hatshepsut knows this, but she wants to go North to honor her grandfather and to find peace in the decision she knows is right. I have agreed because I think it will help the people with the news of her grandfather's passing. I would like you to go with her and make sure she is safe."

"I will. For the love of Egypt and our fathers, I will."

"She is impulsive. She will surprise you every day. She will need to return by the time the body is ready for burial. We will have to have many formal ceremonies at that time. I am hoping to announce the succession, perhaps even a co-regency."

"I will do my best."

"I know you will. That is why I have asked you. I will make sure your family wants for nothing while you are away."

Hatshepsut left in the early morning accompanied by her most beloved attendants. Thutmoses made sure that the most skilled oarsmen were on board. As the barge pulled away, he could see that the captain and his daughter were talking together. He knew she would be safe.

Hatshepsut spent most of the trip sitting on the barge as it made its way north. She always sat looking west. The barge cat sat across her legs and was as still as she. At major population centers the couriers would disembark and pass through the area announcing the coming ascension of Amenhotep as a god. Now and then she and Ramose would talk. He too loved the old stories of Tao, the Brave. Hatshepsut learned the names of all his children and heard firsthand accounts of her father's ferocious battles. One day he spoke of the latest Nubian campaign, "Sometimes your father even scares me. During that last Southern campaign he lashed the dead body of their king to the prow of his ship. No wonder they fear and hate him."

The princess was quiet, then answered, "I guess he doesn't understand that conquering will someday mean ruling and to rule is to do good to the people. That will be hard for the people to forget. I don't think you would have done that. You remind me of my grandfather, strong and kind."

To her surprise he answered, "We are related you know. I am his brother by a lesser wife."

At last the barge arrived at the mini-palace of Amenhotep. Everything was small but elegant. The walls were plastered and covered with red and blue and brown hieroglyphics. The wall in the room that was obviously Hatshepsut's presented the stories of Tao the Brave. Hatshepsut spoke out loud, "My favorite. My bedtime story! Thank you, Pepi." The entry room displayed the last conquests of her father and pictures of the rivers that flowed in the inverted manner from North to South. In the audience room the decoration featured the goddess Ma'at, the goddess of truth. There was room in the palace for Hatshepsut's attendants, but the oarsmen stayed on the barge at the mouth of the wadi. The faithful Ramose, son of Atum, would sleep on the floor near the door of the small palace. Hatshepsut's attendants spoke to each other of the kindness of the old pharaoh and were glad to see the young princess' reaction to the work. After the sun set over the Nile the household settled down to sleep.

In the morning, Hatshepsut gave orders for the day. "After I eat I will read Pepi's wall stories, then I will go bathing. Make arrangement for the attendants to line up along both shores as we did before. In the afternoon I want to visit the craft school that Pepi started. I will select some students to go South. I think he would like that."

Chapter 15:

Argument

While Hatshepsut first went from room to room in the mini-palace admiring the work of her grandfather, a confrontation was going on in a nearby slave home.

"I won't do it. I can't."

"You have to." It was the midwife Puah speaking. "They will kill your whole family including your children. You can choose one or three. The warrior king is fierce. The old Pharaoh is gone. The younger one will not hesitate to kill anyone he sees as an enemy. You should have seen him when he questioned Shiphrah and me about the other children. He had commanded us to kill all the boy babies during birth. He got very angry with us when we told him that the Hebrew women were strong and usually delivered their children before we arrived. Your God gave us the strength to stick to our explanation. Right after that he ordered all Hebrew families to throw their newborn sons into the Nile. You've got to do it. I heard the child last night. It is only a matter of time until someone reports that there is a newborn child here. It is the law. Besides, there are rumors that the royal barge was seen on the Nile yesterday. He may be here now.

"Your God has been good to you. He stopped us from the great sin and gave us the wisdom to answer the rulers. Every time I look at your son there, the one you call the teacher, little Aaron, I know that I did the right thing. He is so clever, so handsome. He speaks Egyptian perfectly, yet he knows your language perfectly as well. Look how well he works with his hands. They have already taught him all the hieroglyphics so he can help carve the plaster on the holy tombs. He was one of the firstborn after that horrible law was given to us midwives. I tear up when I think how close I came to following the evil law. Now the law is after you. They will ask, 'Did you have a child? Was it a boy? Did you throw him in the Nile?' They will know if you lie. You're not a good liar and you know it. You haven't given the baby a name. You know in your heart you have to let him go."

"No. God will give him a name. This trouble cannot be without a purpose. God knows our plight. He will rise up and help us. The great Joseph told us we would someday return to our own land. Perhaps life has to get more difficult so that we will be willing to leave. Our people have lived so many years in this most beautiful part of Egypt. Who would ever want to leave? All the work we have to do, all the injustice of our service may be getting us ready."

"You have to throw him in the Nile. It is the law."

" I do. God does want me to obey the rulers he puts over us. I do have to throw him in the Nile. Thank you, Puah. My mind speaks clearly now."

The good Egyptian woman left the house convinced she had saved her friend's life. She did love those children. They had strange beliefs, but they were good people. Did not Jocobed help her when her own children were born? She herself had two healthy children; all born after the horrible order was given. Jocobed's god had been good to her. She took a deep breath and said to herself. "All will be safe now."

Inside the house Jacobed called to her children. "Aaron, go quickly now and bring me some of that pitch that they use to seal buildings from water damage. Bring it before it cools. Miriam, bring me the strongest of the covered baskets. I know what I need to do." The children watched as she covered the beautifully crafted reed basket with the black gooey tar. "We will do what the Pharaoh commanded. We will cast your brother into the Nile. We just won't let him drown. That would be against the law of God. I am sure that this is what we should do. When anyone asks you if your parents threw your brother into the Nile you can answer truthfully, 'Yes. I saw her do it.' Miriam, when we put your brother in the Nile I want you to follow from the shore to see where it will drift. You are small and it will be easier for you to hide. We will put it in near that place where the river divides and the current is not so strong. There are a lot of bulrushes along the shore and you won't be seen. I will come back here and watch for you and pray. I pray that God will keep you safe and give you wisdom beyond your years."

In the morning Jocobed picked up the basket and placed it on her head as if it were wash or produce. Her children walked on either side. They walked casually from their home and made their way to the river's edge. Jocobed took one last look inside the basket. She placed her hand on the baby's head praying that God would keep him safe and direct his future. She held the basket over the river and gently let it drop into the Nile. "Come Aaron, you and I will return home and Miriam will keep watch."

Back inside the house Jocobed began to recite the story of Abraham and Isaac. She took comfort from the story of her ancestors. She too was offering up her son to the will of God. God had rescued Isaac, telling Abraham, "Now I know that you fear God, seeing that you have not withheld your son from me…And Abraham called the name of the place Jehovah-jira, God provides." She broke off the recitation and offered her own son asking God once again to provide a way.

The Finding of Moses, Painted by
(Juliaan de Vriendt)

Chapter 16:

Rescue

Back at the river Miriam crouched among the dense foliage. The basket drifted steadily down the Nile toward the old temple of Bast. Off in the distance she could see what looked like a merchant barge that carried the bricks her people made to distant building sites. But no, it seemed to have tents, not cargo. As the little basket drifted, she wove her way along the edge of the water. Then she saw the bathing party. It was obvious that the person in the water was important. There were many servants along the sides of the bank. Their eyes followed her movement. They were ready to respond to her every whim. She was a girl or a very young woman. She swam from one attendant to another; it could have been some sort of game. The bather caught sight of the basket in the distance that was now drifting into the rushes.

She signaled to her servants to retrieve the object. She opened the basket and the baby cried. She smiled and said, "This is one of the Hebrews' children. No! It is a gift from Pepi. It is his father Amosis come back to life from the Nile. Pepi sent him to me so that I will not miss him anymore. The Nile gives life. Now I will not be alone. Moses will be my child. I will teach him to chase the sun."

The servants exchanged troubled glances. What would her father think? He was the one who had ordered the death of all the Hebrew boy children. "Princess, you are too young to be a mother."

"Children take a lot of time."

"She's right, how will you feed him?"

"Where will he live?"

Miriam saw her chance. She scrambled to shore and ran breathless toward the assembled group. "Would you like me to go and find a nurse for the child so that she can feed him?"

Hatshepsut didn't hesitate. "Go!" she said. Miriam ran with all her might along the bank.

As she ran she heard, "Are you really sure, princess?"

Miriam burst through the door of her home. "Come mother, the Pharaoh's daughter found the basket. I think she wants to keep the baby. Her servants are trying to talk her out of it. I told her that I could find a nurse to feed the child and she sent me on my way. Let's go."

Mother and daughter ran along the shore. As they ran Jocobed gave thanks for the safety of her son. They slowed before they came to the princess' party to catch their breath. When they arrived Jocobed bowed. Hatshepsut assumed her most royal stance and gave the order. "Take this child away and nurse it for me. I will pay you. He is my son, Moses. Bring him to me at the palace there when he is weaned. Here is a ring with my seal. Show it to anyone who questions you."

The attendants breathed a sigh of relief. At least she won't be taking him to the Southern court. Perhaps she will forget about him. She is just a child herself. Maybe Thutmoses will not find out. Their optimism was short lived. All the way back to the palace and as they dressed her in dry clothes, the princess continued to elaborate how her beloved grandfather had sent his father to her. The Nile had given him back his life in the body of her newfound son. All marveled at the extent of her elaborate imagination. How they loved her. She did miss her grandfather. Perhaps the baby would give her some comfort. Time would tell.

As soon as Miriam and her mother arrived home, Jocobed motioned to her older children to sit near her. "Children, God has answered my prayers. He has given your brother a name. Moses is the name of the pharaohs. It means child in Egyptian. In Hebrew it means draw out. God has drawn your brother out of the Nile. Nothing God does is without a purpose. Perhaps your brother will be the one to draw us out of Egypt and bring us back to our own land as God has promised.

"We can only count on having your brother with us for a short time. We cannot waste a minute. He must learn the holy history. You have been learning all your life. You must help me teach him. He must hear and learn the songs and the generations that are recited over and over again at the new moon festivals.

"We are a special people. We are not special because we are better than other nations. The family of father Abraham was chosen to be the steward of the mysteries of God. The other nations of the world had begun to confuse the work of the creator with the creation. We see this among the Egyptians. They have gods represented by nearly every animal in the world. Each Egyptian worships whichever god has their favorite traits. They have forgotten that there is a God who made everything. All the blessings they say come from

Ra, Amon, Bast, or any of their other 'gods' really come from the God who made it all. God called Abraham to leave his family and start new with a family that would preserve the truth. Abraham was chosen to pass down the history of God with man.

"We are not to change anything. Our ancestor Levi was not given a flattering prophecy from his father Jacob. We must pass it on the way it was given. That is the job of a steward. God's word does not belong to us. We must pass it on and never change it. When we are called on to add to history, we must tell it exactly as it happened. It is our calling. Do you understand? Miriam? Aaron?" She waited for their assent and then continued. "Miriam, begin. Sing the creation song while I nurse your brother."

Her daughter began the familiar song in her beautiful clear voice. "In the beginning, God, he created the heavens and the earth. The earth was without form and void and darkness was upon the face of the deep. And the Spirit of God moved upon the face of the waters."

Within days Jocobed was comforted when she began to hear her young son attempting to join in the singing. "He will learn, smart boy," she said to herself.

Chapter 17:
Resolve

Hatshepsut found peace in the solitude of the miniature palace. The guard her father had sent had become a new friend. She could talk to him. She was surrounded by servants who loved her. They prepared her favorite foods, did her every bidding, and let her rest. The thought of having a son to love sent by her grandfather at her moment of grief was a great comfort to her. How she would love teaching him to chase the sun and to play crocodile.

She knew she had to return to the Southern Palace to honor her grandfather. She watched the Nile and consulted daily with the navigator. She must not be late. She spent the afternoons at the craft school where students were learning how to carve in plaster. She followed the lessons along with the children. She was determined to understand the crafts. She noticed that one boy, one of the Hebrew slaves, was definitely more talented than the rest. As soon as the instructor gave an assignment his hands would fly into action. The other students would stare at their materials and think, wondering how to begin. He would be finished before many of the others started. The instructor and Hatshepsut shook their heads in wonder. Hatshepsut suggested that the talented Hebrew come to Set Ma'at. The instructor said, "He is the best. In the mornings he has been copying the writings on the old tombs for you to take for study at the craft city. He has been very productive. There are two other slaves who also show great ability, Bezaleel and Aholiab. They seem to have been born knowing how to cut precious stones and work in gold and silver to make settings for jewelry. They should go with you. We will miss them but it will be good for Egypt. They will be able to teach others."

Chapter 18:
The "Joke"

When the navigator told Hatshepsut that she needed to get ready to leave, Hatshepsut determined to see her son one more time. She gave orders to her servants to find where he lived. One of the slaves thought that perhaps the midwives would know where a newborn child was kept. They ordered Puah and Shiphrah to the palace. The two good women entered the palace, fearing for their lives. They expected to be chastised by the Pharaoh. To their surprise it was the Princess, the Pharaoh's daughter, not the Pharaoh who sat on the throne, and she addressed them in her most grownup manner, "On the 30th day of the Inundation I arrived at this palace. When I went down to bathe at the Nile, I found my royal son floating in a basket. He is the gift of the gods to me. A dark haired girl told me that she could find me a nurse for my son. The girl brought the nurse to me. She took the child to her home. Before I return to the Southern Palace, I would like to visit my son. Can you find where this woman lives?"

The two women looked at each other. One of them answered, "We know which women are able to nurse a child, we will find the woman for you."

"Take my servant with you. She will report to me and I will visit him today."

The woman bowed. They left the palace followed by Hatshepsut's servant. It was the palace servant who spoke first, "The princess found the child. We know he is a Hebrew child. She is in mourning for her grandfather. We tried to tell her she is too young to be a mother, but no one wanted to say no to her. She insists that the child was sent to her by her grandfather. We, who love her, just want to keep all this from her father. He might not like the idea at all. He was the one who ordered the death of all the Hebrew boys."

Puah answered, "You can count on us to keep this quiet. We think we know who the woman is. We think it is the mother of the child. She has a daughter who would have been staying near her brother to see what would happen. We know the mother very well." As they walked along the midwives glanced at each other as if to say, "Can you believe it?"

When they arrived at the house the two midwives greeted Jocobed with a hug. "The Pharaoh's daughter is planning to come and visit her son some time today. She wanted to let you know. This girl will show her where to come." Jocobed said that the princess was welcome to visit at any time to see her son.

With that the young servant took her leave, "Thank you. I will bring the princess."

The three women stood in silence for a few moments, then they all began to laugh. "So you threw your son into the Nile, did you?"

"Yes I did! Shortly thereafter the princess sent for me to come because she needed a nurse for her son. Look here is her ring to prove that the child belongs to her. When he is weaned, she will take him to live with her in the palace."

"Does he have a name?"

"His name is Moses, like the Pharaohs, Amosis, Thutmoses, Amenmoses. The princess named him. In our language Moses means "Draw out." Our God drew him out of the Nile, saved him from death, and gave him new life. It is not the name I would give to him. If I had to give him a name right now it would be Isaac, which means laughter."

"No one could deny that your god was watching over him. I think I will ask him to watch over my son."

"The boy will learn to read and write and learn all the defensive skills. He will learn about life at court and enjoy the palace life, and I will get paid for taking care of him."

The women all laughed again. The midwives left saying, "We'd better go. I think you are going to have company."

Chapter 19:
Arrangements

Jocobed turned to her daughter. "They are right. Let's straighten up a little bit. We are going to have company. I had better nurse the child so that he will not fuss when Pharaoh's daughter arrives."

Hatshepsut walked faster than her servant. The princess was eager to see her son and hold him again. As they neared the hut, they heard the singing of a young woman. The princess stopped, diverted temporarily from her mission. She wanted to locate the singer. The servant nervously motioned to her, "This way." Fortunately the source of the singing and the home of the nurse were one and the same. The servant knocked, the music stopped, and Miriam pulled back the door covering. The princess entered. Jocobed stepped forward, bowed, and said, "We heard you would come. Here is your son." She placed the baby in princess' arms. There was an awkward moment as the younger woman figured out how to hold the child.

When he was finally settled in the crook of her arm, the young princess studied his face. "He is so beautiful. I forgot what he looked like. I could stay here forever. I have to go back to the Southern palace for my grandfather's funeral ceremonies. I have brought you some money to pay for his care. You will not have to go to work with the other slaves. I want my son to have the best care. I will be back next year to see him again."

When the princess finally looked up, her eyes fixed on the young girl with the dark hair. "Was that you who was singing just now?"

"Yes. I was singing the song about the Voice out of the Whirlwind and about the creation of the world when all the sons of God shouted for joy."

"What is this song?"

Jocobed answered, "It is part of an old story. One that took place long before our Father Jacob came to this land. It took place in Uz far beyond Babylon.

"Babylon! My father has only pressed his soldiers to go as far as Babylon on his last campaign. We have never gone beyond that place. Your people have stories from there? Tell me, I love stories."

"Oh yes! Our Father Abraham lived in Babylon. He was chosen by God to keep all the old stories so that no word of His would be forgotten. God ordered him to leave the place where he was born. He left Babylon and traveled to our own country near what you call the King's Highway, that is used so much for trade. He was given the privilege of preserving the oracles of God."

"Surely those stories are not as old as Egypt. We are the greatest and oldest of civilizations ever."

"You are a great civilization, but our people remember how after the Great Flood the grandson of our Father Noah, Mizraim became your very first ruler, Menes. Our Father Eber whose name we bear was the great-great grandson of the same Noah. So you see we are all one family."

"Our first Pharaoh? Wasn't it Zoser? I am sorry I have to leave tomorrow. I would like to learn more of this history and of the beautiful song."

Just then a breathless Aaron burst through the door saying, "Mother, the Pharaoh's daughter wants to send me South to study. We will leave tomorrow. Some of the other Hebrew children are to go, too."

The princess gave a start and turned in his direction. To her surprise she saw the young boy from the craft school that had so impressed her with his skill. He smiled.

"I know you," she said. "You were at the craft school."

"Yes, princess."

"What is your name?"

"My name is Aaron. I am the oldest in our family."

"I am glad to see you. I will make arrangements for you to live with my good friend, Senenmut, in his house. He is the most gifted of the younger workers. He will teach you wonderful skills. You should see the work he has done for me. Someday he will help me build monuments and temples and even boats to sail on the great water! You will help him."

The princess turned to the mother. "Your children are so blessed by the gods. Your daughter has the most beautiful voice I have ever heard, and your son is the most skilled of all the children in the craft school. I promise he will be well taken care of, and he will learn all the metal crafts. Your son is so gifted. You must be very proud."

" I am proud of all my children. Miriam will sing for you. If you like." She turned to her daughter, "Why don't you sing the promise God gave to Noah?"

Miriam began, "While earth remains these pairs for you
Seedtime and harvest will see you through
Cold and heat, Day and night
Summer and winter before your sight."

Hatshepsut closed her eyes and drifted. When the song finished, she said, "I love the coming of the night. I would like to take my son to watch the sun go down over the Nile. I will carry him. You follow, and you can bring him back here for the night. Perhaps Miriam would like to come and sing for the setting of the sun."

The baby rested quietly in the princess' arms. When they arrived at the small palace, she stopped and sat upon the entry stairs. She spoke softly to the child who look straight into her eyes as if he comprehended every word. "The East is for the living. The West is for the dead. The life-giving Nile lies between. Our houses are on the East bank of the Nile.

The West is set aside for the bodies of the dead. Someday the Nile will rise and those whom Ma'at deems worthy, those who are true and good will have their body parts gathered together to new life…"

She ended the tale by saying, "The Nile did bring new life; it brought me you, my son. Sing, Miriam. Sing about the faithfulness of your god once again."

She looked down, "You, my son, will have more wisdom than anyone. You will learn all the wisdom of Egypt and all the ancient tales as well."

When the sky darkened, the princess kissed the child and reluctantly handed him to Jocobed. "If the winds are not right tomorrow, I will come again but no matter what I'll see you before the next seedtime."

Chapter 20:
Thanksgiving

Once her older children were asleep, Jocobed was overcome with weariness but she knew she couldn't sleep. She took her baby and went outside to her *thoughtful place*. She hadn't been there since the baby was born. She had spent all her time keeping him hidden. Hide the pregnancy; hide the child. What a relief. Thank goodness Miriam had been able to stay with the hidden child when she went to her assignment at the brick factory. Twice a day she would take a little longer than normal to retrieve water from the Nile and slip away to feed the child. Now she could stay home and just see to the child. She breathed a heavy sigh and looked up to the night sky. There they were, all those stars that no man could number. God had said, "Abram, can you count the stars? No! So will be the number of your descendents."

That promise had come true. Abraham and Sarah only had the one child. Now there were so many. Who could count the number of Hebrews just in this area? No one. Who knew how many people there were now in Abraham's family? God was always faithful. Not one of His promises ever failed. She looked up and said aloud, "Thank you for saving my son."

Amram, her husband, was away as usual. When the edict to drown all the boy babies had been given he had declared he would father no more children. He would leave Jocobed so that no more children would be born to such a fate. He would release her from her vows. He didn't know she was pregnant when he left. What a relief it would be to tell him the happy truth. How he will laugh. He will deem it *a Jocobed*, just a joke. He always laughed at her ideas and home improvements. He would say, "Where did you get such an idea?"

She knew what she would answer. "All at once I knew. I needed to obey the ruler, and I needed to obey God. I had to throw him into the Nile. That was the law. Once I resigned myself to do that, I did what was needed to keep him safe. I didn't have a plan beyond that. If night had come...I don't know what I would have done. It's clear that God had a plan and that he put mine into my mind. I am sure that God has a plan for him in the future. God brought Joseph into the court of Pharaoh to save many lives. Now our son will be in the court of Pharaoh. Maybe he will be used to fulfill the promise to our Father Jacob that we will be taken back to our home. This could be the first step in our becoming free. Of course we are free in our souls already." He would surely deem it one of her *jokes*.

They had known one another all their lives. She was the youngest sister of Kohath, Amram's father. So technically she was his aunt, but they were the same age. They had the same family roots. He had liked her because she was different. She loved her family and loved knowing all the family stories. She was one of the few girls in the clan who wanted to recite the family order at the new moon feasts. Girls were not required to participate, but the boys had to recite the family genealogy if they wanted to participate in family discussions. After every monthly meal they would recite, first the oldest, then the next oldest, down to the youngest boy, and then finally any girls who wanted to participate. She had learned the entire Levi genealogy; she often coached the little ones of the family. He knew that she would secretly listen in on the recitation of the other clans. He was not sure, but he suspected that she knew all of them. She was not one to brag. You never knew with her. She taught Miriam the Job saga and all its songs. That was only recited twice a year. She especially liked the narrative tales. You would think she knew Joseph personally. She paid close attention to the last prophecy of Jacob about his children. She was especially aware of the words that had been directed to Levi, the father of their clan. Wasn't she always warning their children to be on guard and to hold their anger in check? He couldn't remember the number of times she had quoted to herself or her children, "Cursed be the Levites anger, for it is fierce." She had even reminded him a few times.

Chapter 21:
Confusion

Back at the mini palace Ramose was not angry. He was confused. The faithful warrior longed for the simplicity of battle. He knew how to drive a chariot while battle raged all around him. This was much more difficult. He had given his word to protect the princess. What was he to do? The attendants had kept the finding of the child to themselves. He had kept his distance when the princess and her servants went bathing. When the midwives arrived, he tried to understand why they were called. When the princess announced the finding of the child and hurried off to the home of the wet nurse, he could do nothing except follow respectfully. The princess gave orders with such authority, he dared not interfere. Pharaoh had warned him that she was full of surprises, but no one could predict this. He kept trying to imagine himself explaining the situation, but could not even form the words in his mind. It was the Pharaoh's law; it was the Pharaoh's daughter. How would he begin to tell him that his own daughter, the one he saw as the hope of the country, had undercut his own decree? For now he would wait. Perhaps his mind would clear before they reached the palace.

In the morning the royal barge was able to catch the wind and begin the sail upstream.

As they left the calmer branch of the wadi, Hatshepsut saw something floating in the distance. As the barge drew near she signaled to her closest servants.

"What is that light colored thing near the shore?" The women stared at the shore then one said, "You don't want to see, princess. It is one of the Hebrew boys who have been thrown in the Nile because of your father's order."

"I do not want to see it, but I will see this law face to face. Bring it to me." Ramose Pi-tum noticed the order and made his way toward the women. He stopped when he got close enough to see and hear what was going on.

The servant tied a line around his waist and reluctantly fought his way to the little body and managed to bring it on board. Hatshepsut took off a silk scarf from around her neck and held out her arms. The decaying boy was handed to her. The servants drew back. Hatshepsut stood still. She stared at the lifeless little body. He was smaller than her son. "He too is beautiful, or he was. Wrap him in the scarf. I want you to bury him in the West when we moor tonight. No child should be thrown away like that. When I am Pharaoh, this law will be no more."

After that she sat silently on the deck watching the river, the actions of the sailors, and the people on the shore. She once again signaled to her servants. "No one is to speak of this to my father. No one is to tell my father about my son Moses. Is that understood?"

Her attendants nodded in assent. None of them wanted to tell the Pharaoh that his daughter had rescued a child from the Nile. In fact many thought silently, *He must never know.*

Ramose Pi-tum, the eye of Horus, watched the scene from a distance. He still could not determine where his duty lay. The lifeless child laid bare the sorrow and grief he had for his own child. He remembered holding his own dead son, the son who could not live. It was obvious that this child from the Nile had not died because it was weak. It had not been sick. It had been a beautiful child. While he mused, he heard another order given by the young princess.

Chapter 22:
Determination

"Tell the navigator to turn back. I will speak to my people. I will do what I can for this law." The oarsmen had to fight the currents, but slowly the barge made its way North toward the small palace. Observers on shore noticed the returning vessel. Word spread quickly, and when the barge landed, there were many to greet the ship. The princess wasted no time. She made her way to the Hebrew forced labor construction site followed by the freed people. She ordered the suspension of work and addressed the people.

"I come in the name of my father, Pharaoh of all Egypt. I am about to return for the celebration of the elevation of my grandfather to the patron deity of the craft city, Set Ma'at. Some of your children are going with me to study there. At that time my father will announce that my brother and I will be his successors. So you see when you see me next, all will know that I am to be Pharaoh along with my brother. I, myself, will return next year to inspect the work you are doing. I am certain that you will provide me with evidence that I can report to my father that you are fulfilling his most important law, the construction of the new store city. The Nile gives us life each year by providing water for our crops. This city will make it possible for us to store abundant crops so we will be prepared for times of drought even as your father, Imhotep, ordered so many years ago. The Nile is a source of life, not death. The gods gave it to our people. The city you build will extend its good. May it bring life and strength to you to do this work. My father regrets that he will not be able to come North to see the work as long as it proceeds on schedule. He is planning several excursions to the South. He will rely on me for the progress reports. I want to report to him that you will work hard to complete this task. I have decided that we will no longer provide you with straw to make the bricks for the cities. You will have to gather that for yourselves after the construction hours. I expect your small children to help in this task. Even your little boys and girls can gather the straw. You will need the help of everyone in your families. Together we will save lives. We will be prepared for any trouble in the future."

She turned and faced the Vizier, the lesser overseers, and soldiers who were present. "This project is so very important that I want you to spend your time on the oversight of this work. I will not question you if the reports on the other laws are not as detailed. This is my ruling." The slaves looked at each other. Was she rescinding the hated law? It sounded like it. A pregnant woman came forward and bowed saying, "We will work hard for you Princess."

The princess placed a hand on the woman's shoulder and said, "Will your child help gather straw?" The woman nodded. "Then we agree. You will build. The Nile will nourish our crops. We will save for times of famine. We will save many lives."

She turned once again to the soldiers. "I will spend one more night in my grandfather's palace and set sail in the morning."

As she made her way back to the palace, she asked for the midwives to come to the palace. When the women arrived, she spoke directly to them, "I do not want you to remind anyone of the law to cast children into the Nile. I am thankful that my grandfather used the Nile to send me my son Moses. The Nile is the source of life not death. Do you understand?"

The women did not understand completely but they nodded as if they did.

"You may go. I will sleep well now."

That evening the news travelled fast. Nearly every sentence contained the words, "Did you hear what the Pharaoh's daughter said?"

The princess spent the trip home planning project after project. She knew what needed to be done. She and her father would work to develop the temple complex. The promised obelisks would be raised. She would make her father love the craft complex and teach him to see the Hebrew workers as individuals and not as a threat to the nation. She would begin a tomb for herself and encourage her father to do the same. She and her half-brother would learn about boats. She would find singers for the temple worship, "singers of Amun." Her father was planning to make another excursion into Nubia. Perhaps the Nile would need to be dredged so that the larger barges could reach those territories. That would take a lot of work. Perhaps her brother could help in that work. There would be no time for her father to go North. He must not go North until he understood that babies were not a threat.

Chapter 23:
Promise

When they arrived back at the palace, Hatshepsut went directly to her father, "Thutmoses and I will be Pharaoh when you are gone. You can announce it. I am not ready to marry just yet. I agree because Pepi would want it to be so."

"He and I discussed it many times. It was his wish."

To himself Thutmoses thought that she seems so grown up, so sure of her words. To his surprise she continued.

"I brought some slave children to study at Set Ma'at. I will take them there in the morning. That was Pepi's wish as well. I think we should form singers for the temple worship. We could call them the singers of Amun. It would be a way of giving grandfather a special honor if there were songs at his service."

"When you get back, Hattie, I would like to go over the plans for the ceremonies. I have also been thinking. We need to begin planning the improvements to the temple complex. Your grandfather and his mother established the craft school. Their vision was to restore the glory of the old Kingdom. You and I will have to carry out their plans."

"Yes, Father, I have been thinking the same. I have some sketches for building on both sides of the Nile. The workers in the North are working hard to fulfill your command to build some storage facilities for abundant crops. The workers seem very motivated."

It was at that moment that captain Ramose decided to keep his peace. He would not speak of the baby Moses. He would not tell why the workers were so motivated. It was a bad law. Too many children died because of disease and weakness. The princess was the Pharaoh's daughter. She did know best in this matter.

Just then Hatshepsut saw the younger Thutmoses entering the palace. He was taller and she thought more handsome than she remembered. She ran to him with obvious excitement. A look of surprise crossed the young man's face when she whispered in his ear. " I have a secret. Promise not to tell anyone?" He nodded slowly and was astonished to hear her continue, "I have a son. Pepi gave me a son. Don't say anything."

Thutmoses witnessed the scene and thought that his daughter must be even more willing to marry than he had previously thought. He walked over to Ramose and said, "Thank you for keeping her safe. She seems to have more ideas than before. What an imagination! I am glad she has agreed to marry Thutmoses. He needs her strength if he is to rule well."

Ramose laughed, "You don't know the half of it. She is amazing. She gives orders as naturally as breathing. She knows how to gain compliance and her servants love her. They call her 'The Pharaoh's Daughter.' When she speaks, they obey."

"It is a good title."

That night Thutmoses slept well. His worries about the succession of the throne were put to rest. The children seemed genuinely fond of each other. Hadn't they gone walking along the river arm in arm, whispering and laughing? The engagement would be announced. He would give them some time, and soon enough they would marry. They were young. Children would follow. The dynasty would endure.

His son was not so comforted. He had tried to understand what Hatshepsut had said to him. The story she had told him was intermingled with her insistence that her grandfather had placed a child in the Nile for her to find. It seemed clear to him that she had stumbled upon a Hebrew child, who had been thrown into the Nile because of his father's law. How had it lived? She thought the child was hers. What would she do with a child? The child was obviously that of slaves! What would their father think? What would their father do if he found out? He hated and feared those Hebrew people. What could be done? Maybe she would forget. The child would live with its nurse and all would be over. He was not going to bring up the subject again. She was talking of revising the temple complex. She talked of shipbuilding and of the funeral preparations. All these things would help her to forget. He could only hope. The whole thing made him nervous. He wasn't about to argue. In fact, he only ever argued with Hatshepsut twice in his life.

The patron god and goddess of Set Ma'at,
Amonotop (Hatshepsut's Pepi) and his mother (The Great Mother)

Chapter 24:
Set Ma'at

Hatshepsut had visited the craft village with her grandfather and her mother. She had taken it as it was, but now she set her mind to making it what it was meant to be. At breakfast with her father she began. "Now about Set Ma'at. Grandfather and the Great Mother hoped it would restore the glory of Egypt. That cannot happen unless it is the best place in the world for artists to work. The houses are of good size, but we need to make sure that each one has stairs to the roof so that the family can sleep outside when it is too hot. Every building should be studied so that the structure will not block the breeze down the valley. The main roads will have to be covered. When the Nile floods, we need to divert some of the water to make sure there is a good supply there when the water recedes. There should be an entry arch with the figures of Pepi and his mother and the story of the building of the city. The pillars of the roof can document the building projects."

"Wait a minute princess, you are going too fast for me. It sounds good, but I think I have to write this down."

Egyptian House(Constance Baikie)

The princess took a deep breath and began again, "The workers should be given land for their own tombs. That will increase their skill level, and all their work will be better. We will have to give them servants to help with laundry and carrying water. We can't waste their time on things like that."

"How have you thought of all of this?"

"I have been thinking of it for years. When they work on the Mortuary Temple it will be too far for them to travel each day. The walls will have to be covered with history. We will have to make a camp for them and make arrangements for food to be brought to them. They will have to have time off. Maybe two teams would work. What do you think?"

"I need to think for a moment. What Mortuary Temple? You and I should visit the city and you can show me what you mean. How much of all of this needs to be done before the ceremonies for your grandfather?"

"We should at least have the arch constructed and have the plaster carved with the images. I think Pepi should be enthroned as Amenhotep of the Town and the Great Mother as The Lady of the West. How do you like those titles? Every year we can have a festival and celebrate the additions to the city."

"My daughter, I am a man of war. I think you indeed have the spirit of the Pharaohs. It takes my breath away, but I can begin to see what you are talking about. I can see the glory that your grandfather intended. Tell me more."

"We should find the best singers to be the singers of Amun. I'm sure they had singers in the Old Kingdom. They can sing at all the ceremonies. Grandfather will like to hear the singing as he makes that great journey. Music has sometimes made me feel I am in a different world."

"Singers?"

"I told you. We must have singers for grandfather's burial. We need dancers too. We need them not only for funeral ceremonies, but also in the land of the living. Wouldn't it be nice to hear music at the rising and setting of the sun? I promised Pepi that I would raise obelisks, one for him and one for me to face the west and honor the gods. You will want to raise one too. I saw some stone along the Nile that is red in color. Don't you think we should build a Red Chapel in the temple complex? I think we should."

"If we do all this building, how will I secure the borders?"

"Don't worry father, I can work with Ineni. He is a great builder. He will understand what we mean. He doesn't need to be watched every step of the way. We can count on him to carry out our plans. Then there is our kinsman Senenmut. Remember the cat he carved for me? He already knows about many of my ideas for the Mortuary Temple. I know he could direct a team of his own. He is also a good teacher. His pupils are nearly as good at carving as he. We can do it. We just have to begin. I want to make arrangements for one of the slave children to live in his house. Of course his house would have to be made larger, maybe a double house that shares a common area. The slave I have in mind will learn quickly. He did a lot of the work on the mini-palace. It will be the start of Senenmut's team.

"Father, when you go South, I think you should take some of the workers with you. It would be good if we dredged the Nile so that the barges can go further. That would open more trade with those people. If we trade with them, there is less a chance that they will turn against us."

Thutmoses continued to nod as his daughter spoke but he didn't hear any more of her elaborate plans. Her ideas came too fast for him to take in. More important to him was the relief he was feeling. A great weight had lifted from his heart. She had agreed to marry. The succession would be secure. She was even helping him see his way forward in the ruling of the people. Her ideas were concrete; they would build up the kingdom. He would work with her to rule. He would treat her almost as Pharaoh as her father has treated him. When he was gone, his son would work with her as well. That boat project would be a good starting place for the two of them. He himself would have to instruct him in the art of war. He needed to be a better soldier. After the funeral they would go South, maybe dredge the Nile a bit and open trade like Hatshepsut said. His son would lead a division. Yes, that was the next thing. He would ask Ramose Pi-tum to drive his chariot. He would be safe enough if anything went wrong. A good plan.

Chapter 25:
Nurse

Meanwhile Jocobed's life fell into a happy routine. She missed her older son, but was sure that he too was safe in the protection of God. When her husband returned, she was prepared to explain her plan to him. Her older children and friends understood her rules. No one was ever to refer to her as mother. She should always be referred to as *nurse*. The name *mother* must be reserved for the young princess. In a year Hatshepsut would return. The boy must not draw back from her as from a stranger.

As the child grew, she made sure that he heard the family stories in Hebrew. She was also careful to speak naturally to him in Egyptian. She was thankful for her friendship with her Egyptian midwives. Their families continued to prosper and the women visited quite frequently. The little Moses was a favorite with everyone. She told her son the Joseph tales in Egyptian as well as in Hebrew. She fought against her own instinct to keep to herself and willingly watched neighbors' children so that she could ask them to take care of her son in return. She had always taken her other children with her but he needed to accept care from those he did not know. Sometimes she went so far as to use that strange eye makeup. "What are you doing now?" her friends would ask.

"We're practicing!" was her ready reply.

The child grew quickly. Soon he was singing along with his sister. One day Jocobed had another idea. She carefully constructed another oral tradition for her son. It was the tale of the drawing out of the Nile. She recited it regularly. She always finished with, "Your mother is a beautiful Egyptian princess. She saved your life. You should always be thankful to her."

Pharaoh (Constance Baikie)

When the wife of the Vizier extended an invitation to her home, she accepted gladly and rejoiced when her son smiled at the great lady, walked up to her with open arms saying, "Mother?" She knew he would be ready.

The young Hebrew mothers would often turn to her. She would help with care for the children that were too big to be carried to work but too small to be left with the group nurses. She did her best to encourage the mothers. One young mother from the clan of Judah had named her son Caleb. One day Jocobed's temper got the best of her. She challenged the mother, "Why would you call your child Caleb? It means dog!"

The mother responded, "His life will be that of a dog. Worse. What future does he have? You saved your child and you made it possible for the rest of us to keep ours but what good is it? We have no hope."

Jocobed was quick to answer, "Don't you pay attention to the prophecies about your family. When I was a little girl, I wished I were from the Judah clan. What a promise you have! My family has a curse on our anger. You! You have a promise of a king! The scepter shall not depart from Judah, nor a lawgiver from between his feet, until Shiloh come. I haven't heard of anyone named Shiloh coming, have you? Your family has the best of all the promises. Why would you call your son, *dog?*"

At this she picked up the small boy, sat him in her lap and said, "You, my child, are from a royal line. Someday, someone from your family will be the king of all our people. Someday God will take us back to our own land. You must learn all you can so that you can serve. God has a great promise for you."

The boy looked directly into her eyes without blinking as she spoke, and he continued to watch her long after she set him back down. After that he was the most attentive of all the children in his clan; he was quick to memorize the recitations given at the new moon festivals. Jocobed was careful to recite the common tales when he was in her home.

An Egyptian Chariot(Constance Baikie)

Chapter 26:
Funeral

What the Ancient Egyptians believed: The god of the dead, Anubis, stands with the departed by a scale where the heart of the person is weighed against one feather from the crown of Ma'at, the goddess of truth and justice. If the person is judged good and just, he will be accepted into fellowship with the god Osiris.

While Hatshepsut had been making her pilgrimage North, her grandfather's body was being prepared to become a mummy. It took seventy days before they could honor him with the funeral ceremonies. The body needed to be dried. This took forty days. All the organs that would deteriorate quickly were removed and preserved in jars. Skin, hair, and muscles could be dried in place. Packets of salts from the Nitrian wadi in the North were placed inside the body cavity that had been emptied of all organs except for the heart, which was believed to be the center of intelligence and being. The salts were also packed around the body. The salts drew out the moisture from the body. After the drying process the body was be treated to make it have some flexibility again. Once again the body was washed with wine and then a variety of oils were applied. During this time the priests offered ritual prayers on behalf of the dead. The empty body cavity was packed with linen so that the body would retain its shape.

Next, linen strips were used to wrap the body. Occasionally amulets were wrapped in the bandages. Once the body was completely wrapped a painted mask with the features of the dead was placed over the face. More bandages held it in place.

During this time the coffins were also completed. Personal information was added to the decorations. Furniture and other supplies were brought to the tomb to be buried with the dead so that he would have what he needed in the afterlife.

Finally the time came for Pepi's funeral and enthronement. The location of the old pharaoh's mortuary temple and his tomb dictated the route of the funeral procession. The royal family began the festivities by passing through the gate and praying at the chapel that Amenhotep had constructed in the land of the living.

Chariots took the family to the place where Hatshepsut and her grandfather had stopped to watch the setting sun. Hatshepsut held out an arm to the setting sun. Her family followed her example. They took a boat over to the West and proceeded to the mortuary temple. There the priests performed the ceremony of opening the mouth by touching the mouth and various other parts of the body so that the soul would be free to come and go at will. After the prayers were made, only the most trusted servants and family members proceeded to the secret burial chamber. The mummy was placed in a decorated coffin. That coffin was placed in a larger coffin, and finally placed in a rectangular box. The accumulated objects were packed around the room. The room was sealed, and the mummy was left to face the judgment of the gods. His heart would be weighed against a feather of the goddess Ma'at, the goddess of truth and justice. If he passed the test, he would be welcomed among the gods. Hatshepsut was not anxious about her grandfather. He had always loved truth and there was nothing he wanted more than justice among the Egyptian people. The next day the entrance to the craft city was adorned with a statue of the dead Pharaoh sitting on a throne, watching over his beloved city. Hatshepsut continued to offer prayers to her beloved Pepi for the rest of her life.

Chapter 27:
Planning Ahead

When the formal ceremonies ended, Hatshepsut did not stop planning. She worked with abandon at the craft center. She made sure of shaded walkways, water delivery systems. She had Senenmut's house enlarged, or rather she had a second dwelling built beside it with a connecting common chamber. Her plan was to have the nurse come to live there with her children, the artist and the singer. Moses could live there too if she couldn't find a way to have her father understand Pepi's gift.

When a year had passed from the passing of the Pharaoh, the Old Mother's body finally gave way and new funeral procedures were begun. Hatshepsut once again traveled North promising to return for the ceremonies for her great-grandmother. The night before she left she promised her father that she would wed Thutmoses after the mourning time for the Great Mother had passed. She said she would be ready. She promised that she would bear all the news to the noble families. Ramose again accompanied her, hoping that the question of the Hebrew child would resolve itself. She fell into the habit of talking with the soldier as the sun set. They calculated that he was sort of a great uncle to her. Her agile mind reached the conclusion quickly, "If my grandfather had died as a young child as his older brother did, you might have been Pharaoh now." The soldier laughed, "I would rather serve Pharaoh than be Pharaoh. Your grandfather had other brothers. No one can say what would have been. I am content. I do love Egypt and share my brother's dream to restore it to its former glory. I am glad when I see how the people love you. You have gained their trust."

Ramose watched at each stopping point as Hatshepsut greeted the people. Now she had the demeanor of a queen. A calm and steady grace replaced the childlike brooding that had been present after her grandfather's death. When the pyramids were visible in the distance, she began to speak of the child she had been given by the Nile. Any hope that Ramose had had that she would forget died away. He began to steel himself for what was to come.

As soon as the barge landed, the princess made herself ready to visit her son. She had a small robe and a basket of fruit to take with her. She took a female attendant with her and Ramose followed at a distance. She had no trouble finding the small home. News of the barge's arrival had reached the whole region. The princess knocked at the door. Miriam answered. When the princess stepped inside, a dark haired toddler turned to face her. He took a step back, looked inquisitively at Jocobed, and questioned, "My mother?" She nodded. The child went straight forward, paused and made an almost imperceptible bow. The princess opened her arms and the child rushed forward with his arms up in the air. He hugged her neck and kissed her on both cheeks.

Hatshepsut offered the child a date. The child took the date and took it to his nurse. She showed him how to take a small bite. He returned to the princess, smiled, and put out his hand. She gave him another. She said, "I loved these as a child. My mother tells me I loved them too much. I still enjoy them, especially when I am trying to think through a problem." The child didn't give her time to continue. Her attention was diverted as he climbed into her lap and began happily to nibble on the fruit. So the ritual began. The child would nibble on the new treat, stop, look at it, lean out, look the princess in the eye, smile, and wait until she smiled and nodded at him. Then his attention turned once more to the date. Finally the child leaned back against her body. Instinctively the young woman began to rock the child. Soon she felt the weight of his head as he fell asleep in her arms. She continued to rock him in silence, enjoying the feelings that waved over her. She whispered to Jocobed. "I have promised my father that I will marry when I return to the South."

The older woman answered, "You seem too young."

"Nevertheless Egypt needs me to marry. There can be no time when the succession to the throne is not clear. That is what my grandfather said and I am sure he was right."

There was silence for a while, then the princess continued, "The time will come when I bear children myself. I will need a nurse. I want you to serve as nurse to my children. You would have to move to the area of the Southern Palace."

"Your older son is living with my kinsman, craft master, Senenmut. I have enlarged his house adding a second dwelling, which is much larger than what you have here. Come South and you can have your children together in one place. Aaron could continue with his craft service and your daughter here could work with the young singers."

She paused and looked down at the sleeping child. "He has grown so much. I know he is not yet weaned, but by this time next year he will be changed again. I wish I could rock him this way every day and see him grow. Maybe you could move now?"

Ramose heard this part of the conversation from his place at the door of the house. A sense of dread came over him. Her father would surely find out about the child. What would happen then? Thutmoses would be furious. He would think it treason. The good man began to fear for his own family.

The princess seemed to read his mind. He heard her say, "My father does not know about Moses. I was afraid that he would not understand the gift I had been given by the Nile. I will be taking many workers back to the craft city. He will be pleased that I am bringing a nurse for children I may have. He will know I am serious about continuing the line of the

Pharaohs. If he asks, I will tell him that you are nurse to a child of a noble family and that all have agreed that you could come South with me. He need not know that I am the noble family! I'll wait until he loves the child as I do. I think Moses could even join in the beginning lessons and start to learn to read. He is so bright. It is hard to believe that he is what? A year and a half old?"

The soldier began to breathe steadily again. Perhaps she knew what she was doing. It would be a dangerous move, but the princess was certainly skilled at getting things done. He would try not to worry. At least the princess was not going to do anything too dangerous. Maybe it was rash, but then again the king would never think that she was returning with a child given to her by her grandfather in the Nile. No, he would never suspect that.

Chapter 28:
The Move

Ramose was right. The move was made. When Hatshepsut returned with her normal flurry of activity, her father never noticed the small child. So it was that Moses, Jocobed, Aaron, and Miriam lived in the royal craft city. Aaron continued to learn more of the metal crafts and Miriam taught the children of the craftsmen to sing. Moses was sent to school, the craft school, where he too learned to read and write the hieroglyphic alphabet. He learned quickly the skills his brother had mastered so well. In addition he learned the intricate embroidery techniques. In the years to come Hatshepsut would spend many an hour in the common area between the two dwellings. Here she worked with Senenmut making building plans and, of course, seeing her son. Here she talked openly with everyone. It was a safe place for her. Here she relaxed. She could be herself. She loved the Hebrew songs and stories and compared the teaching of the ancient religion with that of the Egyptians. Her father did think that she spent too much time at the craft center. There were rumors that she was romantically involved with Senenmut. He didn't believe them himself. He knew that when she was at the main palace she and his son were busy with their own plans. She just threw herself completely into the activities at hand. He never suspected that the other family, the family of Senenmut's apprentice, concealed her most precious secret, that of her son.

The funeral ceremonies for the Great Mother paralleled that of her son. Once again the procession passed through the temple to the mother's tomb. Her seated statue was placed opposite that of her son in the craft city. The pillars behind them recorded the history of the complex and the promise of accomplishments to be restored. Throughout the ceremonies Thutmoses walked arm in arm with his daughter. Her presence gave him a sense of stability. He whispered to her that the singing at this funeral was sweeter to hear than that which had been sung at her grandfather's funeral. He even complemented her choice of a teacher of the children.

Chapter 29:
Wedding

Hatshepsut turned her mind to planning the wedding. All the noble families of Egypt were invited to the celebration and the crowning of the young people. The older Thutmoses felt glad that the succession was being made more secure. The younger Thutmoses was overcome with the prospect of the marriage. He had loved the girl from the first moment he saw her. He would do whatever she said. He couldn't believe that she was to be his wife. He would even keep that secret that had something to do with a child from the river.

While Hatshepsut planned the wedding, her father turned his mind to military matters. He felt the need to make a show of force and will. He wanted to finish with the Southern military campaign to quiet any fears that the people might have about the ability of his son to hold power. He personally worked every day to train his son. The boy was not a great fighter, but he did not hesitate to try. Ramose would certainly have to watch over him, too. He would make sure he was the driver for his son's chariot. There were so many tasks for that good man. If they could come home with a victory and promise of tribute from the Southern neighbors, all would be well.

The funeral celebrations were elaborate, but they were nothing compared to the royal wedding. First the palace was remodeled to make new living quarters for the young couple. The princess chose to have her private quarters in the area formerly occupied by her great grandmother, the Great Mother, whom she admired so much. The walls were painted with the same stories her grandfather had placed in the small northern palace. The floors were covered with cedar planks.

A spiral staircase led to an opening in the ceiling that made it possible for her to sit above her own bedroom and see the stars. The prince's quarters adjoined hers and were where Pepi's apartment had been. The throne room was outfitted with a series of cleverly placed thrones that would impress foreign visitors. When the day of the wedding arrived, flowers adorned every step leading up to the palace. The bank of the Nile was lined with children. The procession went just as the princess had envisioned. She began at the home of Senenmut. Her secret family helped her get dressed. Jocobed hovered over her like a mother. Senenmut made sure that every jewel was perfectly set. Miriam sang the song of beginnings to her as she dressed. She wore a filmy white dress woven with gold threads. Her head and neck were adorned by a beaded collar and crown of gold and lapis lazuli. As she left the craft city she paused, turned and spoke to the patron god and goddess of the city, "Help me Pepi. Help me Great Mother. Help me to lead your people with wisdom and strength. Help Twoey to become the Pharaoh he needs to be. Protect Moses. Restore glory to Egypt as I know you desire."

As she prayed, the craftsmen gathered round her. Most carried palm branches or flowers. They followed her chariot down to the Nile where one of the more ornate high prow boats, that she and Twoey had designed and built, was moored. The sail was not visible as the boat was going to be carried by the current. A lone helmsman was hidden among the foliage aboard the craft. He would keep the boat on course. A heron was released. He gave a screeching cry, rose up and soared South over the Nile to a nesting area far beyond the palace. The wedding guests looked up in unison at the graceful flight, their hearts lifted by the beautiful blue color of its wings. When they once again looked down, they saw the princess standing in the bow of her vessel. The sunlight reflected off each gold thread, surrounding her in a great whirlwind of light. The jewelry glowed with the heavenly blue color. Her dress fluttered behind her, bright and shining. She stood straight and tall. She raised her left arm to salute the dead. Then her right to embrace the living. All eyes followed her gliding along while she held her arms outstretched as if to embrace the whole world, the living and the dead. Slowly the floating vessel made its way toward the palace. Hatshepsut had long ago won the hearts of her people so that nearly all the noble families sent representatives to the event. All eyes were fixed on her.

Now it was Twoey's turn. No one noticed when he stepped into a second boat. It was his favorite. It was under sail, and he himself took the rudder. The sail caught the wind, and the boat moved toward the center of the Nile. He knew what he was doing. This was his greatest skill. He was not a very good archer. He wasn't a great swordsman, but he could control his ship. He too wore white adorned with gold and lapis lazuli. His crown was the complement of Hatshepsut's. He skillfully sailed his vessel past that of the princess. The two saluted each other. He turned the boat in a graceful arch and brought it about so that the ships were side by side. As they approached the palace, the two vessels came into port together. Twoey sprang from his place, he passed the rope off to an attendant, then extended his arm to help Hatshepsut step out of her vessel. The princess seemed to glide forward. Together they climbed the stairs from the river to the portico.

The viziers of most of the regions of Egypt were there. Nobles and officials stood to witness the event. For years afterwards they would ask new acquaintances, "Did you see the wedding of the Pharaoh's daughter?"

If the answer was negative, the newcomer was bombarded with descriptions of her beauty, the skill of the young prince, and expressions of hope for the future. "Those young people have vowed to make Egypt competitive on the open sea. I'm sure they will. You should have been there."

The actual marriage ceremony was short. Priests from various cults chanted their blessings. After the vows were made, Thutmoses himself placed new crowns on the heads of the couple as a public demonstration that they were, in fact, the intended next rulers. When the young couple retired to the marriage chamber, the crowd cheered. The music and feasting continued well into the night. Thutmoses was relieved. He had done what he could for the succession. He had kept faith with his father. Surely they would have children.

Hatshepsut's Obelisk
(photo credit: Dave Howe)

Chapter 30:
Heirs

The older Thutmoses was not disappointed. When the time came to take his son South for the military campaign, Hatshepsut announced that she was with child. Thutmoses thought that if they could just return with victory in hand that all would be well. He could finally stay put and watch the workers build his temple complex and add to the building on the East side of the Nile as well. How he longed for a rest. There was so much building to be done.

Hatshepsut spent about a month in the craft village. She enjoyed the attentions of Jocobed, who answered her questions about her coming delivery. She returned to the palace and fell into a routine of watching for signs of the warriors' return. She was excited on the day that she saw the dust rising in the distance, swirling in the wake of the returning soldiers. They were flying a flag of victory. She alerted her attendants, and when the soldiers arrived, she greeted each one with a thank you. A servant gave each one a fragrant orange to quench their thirst. She looked eagerly for her old friend Ramose, but did not find him driving her husband's chariot.

When she asked after him, she was told the awful truth. The heavy bow had proved too hard for the prince to manage. The enemy moved first. Her husband's life was in danger. Ramose had pushed the young ruler down, but had been hit himself.

"He's dead? It cannot be."

"He prayed as he was dying. I heard him cry out to Isis."

" No, don't you know! He was calling out to his wife! His last thought was concern for what would happen to her and their children. He always thought of others and Egypt before himself."

"Perhaps she will marry again."

"Of course she will. You will have to marry her!"

The first real argument between the two new rulers began.

"But we are married. I don't want another wife."

"You have to marry her. How will the people know that their loyal service will not be taken for granted? It is the only way you can provide for her needs, keep her safe, and care for his children. It's the least you can do."

"What!"

"Don't you know anything? That's why rulers have harems. If you take a daughter of a potential enemy to wife, they will not attack. If you take to wife the widow of a brave soldier, other soldiers will not fear the battle. You don't have to see her every day. Build a nice complex for her family where she can be safe. The nicer you make it the better. Tell him, Father."

Her father stood still, perplexed. He had never understood the harem. He knew his mother was a lesser wife. Is this how he came to be born? What expedient had caused his father-in-law to marry his mother? He had married Hatshepsut's mother because the pharaoh had practically commanded him. He hadn't thought about what he was doing or why. Hatshepsut spoke with such certainty. Is this how the main wife dealt with the existence of other wives?

Hatshepsut continued, "You have to give his family all the protection he would have given them. He died for you! There is no other way."

Finally the father responded, "Ramose was the most faithful servant. You should do this for him. She has many children who need to be cared for. It would be wrong to leave her to fend for herself."

Hatshepsut added to the idea, " Perhaps we should name something after him as well. The blood of the pharaohs was in his veins. His name should be remembered. Maybe someday a pharaoh will be named after him."

The younger Thutmoses was not enthusiastic, but he understood what his wife was telling him. He left the palace to find Isis to tell her of her husband's bravery and to assure her of his protection. She paled at the news, understood his offer of support, and, to his surprise, put her arms around him, leaned her head on his chest and sobbed. He held her close. The desire to protect her became a reality. He vowed to himself to do what Hatshepsut had insisted. He immediately gave orders to the builders construct an addition to the palace that would make it possible for her family to have privacy if they so desired, but with access to the common rooms of the palace as well. He would make it more welcoming than the complex he had known as a child.

When he told Hatshepsut of his plans, she had only one thing to add, "I've been thinking about what we should name after him. How about the store cities up North? That would remind the people of his service, and honor him at the same time. He was there when we started the project; it would preserve his name into the future."

The addition of Isis and her five sons to the palace complex brought unexpected changes to daily life. The boys were all strong and spent a great deal of time out of doors. When their father was alive, they strove to excel at military arts. This they continued. A covered walkway was constructed to protect their comings and goings to the training camps of the army. Now that they were part of the royal household, they were expected to excel at reading and writing as well. At first they progressed slowly at the new skills, but soon they could be seen examining the writings on the pillars and colonnades. They descended upon the palace pool where they enthusiastically competed with each other in impromptu races. Thutmoses II was glad to see that they did not have to hide from the first family as he had when he was a boy.

Hatshepsut was determined to finish as many of her construction projects as she could before her child was born. The obelisk to honor her grandfather had been raised. Another was to be raised next to it to commemorate the love she had for him. She found that she took pleasure in visiting her grandfather's monument praying, "See, Grandfather, I honor you today." She ordered the construction of a small chapel east of the two obelisks for a private chapel. When Senenmut suggested that it be made of the red marble they had found, she was delighted. "That will make it extra special." Her tomb was nearly complete although she had begun to wish she had chosen another location. There was not room for the chariot ramps she had envisioned as a child. Maybe she would build another tomb later.

Her father also turned his mind to building. His vision was to unify the temple complex. A series of pylons around the area where flags could be mounted added the look he envisioned. He began to understand. The people needed to have help visualizing the greatness of their civilization. The heat of the desert motivated him to build a forest on the complex, a forest of cedar pillars. The shade and perfume of the wood provided visitors to the complex with a reprieve from the heat. He had two obelisks raised to commemorate his reign. He had to keep pace with his daughter's example. More and more the father looked to his daughter for guidance in the great adventure of being the Pharaoh, the father of his people. When it came to his son, his hope was that he would continue to listen to his wife. Perhaps his warrior skills could be developed if they all joined the sons of Isis during morning training sessions. He was glad that the two younger rulers continued with their boat project. They were now talking about building a fleet with each ship requiring thirty rowers. Nothing like that had ever been built in Egypt before. Hatshepsut kept explaining how it would impress the people when those ships sailed and how it had to be a success. War and trade were essential to any great kingdom.

Chapter 31:
Motherhood

Hatshepsut was young, perhaps too young, to become a mother. The labor began earlier than expected. When the time came, the delivery brought its own set of problems. Jocobed was there, ready to take the child, and become nurse to it as promised. The midwives attended the princess at the birthing stools. Several other mothers came after Hatshepsut; the cry of new life could be heard and still Hatshepsut's labor continued adding to the anxiety she was feeling. At last the child was born. It was a girl.. Hatshepsut's named her "Beauty (Neferure)." The child's eyes were open, and she looked straight into her mother's eyes. The tiny lips were beautifully arched and delicate. Then the young mother lost consciousness. She was losing too much blood. Her face was pale and translucent.

Jocobed wrapped the child and turned to attend the mother. For the rest of the day and through the night, she tended mother and child. She spooned liquids into the mother, who gradually regained consciousness. Delirium and fever came with the blood loss.

Whenever the younger woman came to herself, she would cling to the older woman, "Where is Beauty? Is she all right? Stay with me. Don't leave me." Jocobed would quiet her fears.

In the morning she was much better. The young mother insisted on holding her child. She held the child close to her face and began to tell her the story of her older brother and how he was the gift of her grandfather. She plied Jocobed with orders. "You must have Miriam sing to her like you did with Moses. My son is the best child I have ever seen. Teach Beauty, too! Teach her all the old stories."

Hatshepsut: The Pharaoh's Daughter

Word was sent to the palace that she was out of danger. Hatshepsut's father felt a great weight lifted. He wished the child had been a boy, but he thought he would enjoy another royal princess. Maybe he and she could renew the custom of chasing the sun. The people still talked about those days. More than anything he was grateful that Hatshepsut had not joined her departed brother and sister. What would he do without her?

Not long after, Isis also went into labor. This time everything went smoothly. The experienced mother delivered a healthy baby boy. Dare they call him Thutmoses III? Father and son took a long walk along the Nile and decided they would.

When Hatshepsut and Isis were settled in their palace apartments, Thutmoses I surprised everyone by hastily planning a public appearance on the outer portico. He didn't consult with his daughter. He was thinking about the people and their perception of the royal family. He had an idea. He was sure it was a good idea; in fact, he was proud of it.

After a quick trip to the craft village, Thutmoses ordered the palace singers and dancers to parade throughout the area to attract a crowd. Rumors of the new child and the singing parade drew nearly everyone out into the street to see what was happening. The dancers made their way up the staircase to the portico. Pharaoh himself wearing his most impressive military regalia appeared carrying the two babies. Each of the babies was wearing a delicately wrought golden crown. The crowd went wild, cheering. The few people who didn't follow the parade heard the report. "You should have seen the little prince and princess! Little Pharaoh and his Little Wife."

When the event was described to Hatshepsut, she smiled politely, but she didn't laugh. She leaned over and whispered into her husband's ear and said, "I have a son. Just remember, he whom Beauty chooses will be Pharaoh." It was a sentence she would repeat often when the two of them were alone.

Chapter 32:
Stability

Thutmoses who was now a grandfather of two children was content. He thought that even Amenhotep would have been happy. The people would have assurance of the rulers to come. Military action had secured the peace to the South and East. A second campaign revealed that Thutmoses II had become a better soldier. Another definite victory! Egypt was on her way to the ancient glory. The architects had rediscovered many of the old building techniques, and the new monuments were making the older buildings look better. Hatshepsut had so many building ideas; she would take care of that. And the boat project was coming along. Trade across the great water would bring unprecedented riches. If Thutmoses III grew up to be anything like his five brothers, what a leader he would be. Maybe the next project should be to rework the training complex. The best soldiers would be put in charge of the training of the young Pharaoh. He would consult with his men as soon as he could and see if any of them had suggestions to make. The improvements at the craft city had brought about a skill of workmanship that made all the building and textile work the envy of the world. The same needed to be done for the military arts.

Chapter 33:
Setback

The soldiers did have ideas. They suggested a more orderly arrangement of facilities. A rough track for practicing chariot driving was needed. They all agreed that targets to shoot at from a chariot in motion needed to be built at a safe distance from bystanders. Climbing poles for the younger boys would strengthen their arms for future bow use. Wrestling should be taught at all ages. A variety of detailed drawings were made and discussed. Thutmoses selected ten of the planners to visit the current training area to see what should be preserved and what needed to be changed.

As they walked around the complex, it became very clear that the current layout was haphazard. Some older children were trying to shoot arrows from a chariot at a target mounted on a bale of hay. That was something that definitely needed changing. That whole area needed to be well away from the other trainees. Maybe a wall was needed between the archers and the wrestlers. They all agreed to the change.

The decision was a good one, but it came too late. As the planners turned away from the archers, a chariot wheel slipped into a gully, the archer lost control of the bow, and an arrow shot wildly into the air struck the Pharaoh in the back. Panic ensued. Physicians were called. The wounded Pharaoh was carried to the palace. The arrow was removed, but the damage was done.

Hatshepsut rushed to her father's side. She stayed with him for days while he lingered between life and death. The wound became infected, and his breathing became labored. Over and over he mumbled, "I should have listened more to you. I am not ready. My son is not ready. Send for him. You will have to help him be Pharaoh. Together you will be Pharaoh. Promise me." When Thutmoses II arrived, he reached for his arm and held on, "Listen to your wife. She will make you Pharaoh, just as my wife made me Pharaoh. Be strong. Be strong. Make sure of the succession. Protect the people." Soon his old fears returned, "My tomb is not ready! I'm not prepared to go. I should have finished my tomb. What will happen to me? What will happen to my body? I'm not ready."

Hatshepsut assured him, "You will be able to finish your tomb. You are going to get better."

When she heard the sound of the death rattle in his voice she finally said, " Don't worry, Father, you can have my tomb. It is ready. I will build another one."

Thutmoses heard her. He relaxed and slept. He slipped peacefully into the next life. Hatshepsut was shaken, but she took charge. Her tomb was modified to memorialize her father's accomplishments. All the changes were made before the mummy was completed.

Chapter 34:
Troubled Partnership

Though shocked by the death of the young and powerful Pharaoh, the nation was not shaken when Thutmoses II and Hatshepsut took power. The young couple was popular. The people had always loved their Pharaoh's daughter. They had seen the skill of Thutmoses in handling the boat on the Nile.

Hatshepsut had always thought of herself as a ruler, and she had plans. She was determined to continue military excursions to the East and South to facilitate trade and peace. She officially rescinded the order that required that the male children of slaves be cast into the Nile though no one really took notice because the law had been neglected for so long. She had many building projects underway and she would build another more elaborate tomb now that her father's mummy was in her first tomb. She and Thutmoses had decided to make a fleet of ships to sail on the open water. The small models were working and stayed afloat when they simulated ocean storms in the palace swimming pool. They had decided on the design of the sails. Of course most importantly the craft city would continue to produce skilled workers and transcribe the ancient writings. Egypt would recover her old glory just as her grandfather had dreamed.

Thutmoses was not so confident. He knew she had plans. He also knew the great argument was coming. He dreaded it from the moment his dying father had advised him to listen to his wife. "She will make you Pharaoh," he had said. He did not want to argue with his wife. He would agree to most anything she asked, but not everything. She had been right about their last argument. It had been right for him to marry Isis. The loyalty and affection of the troops was proof of that decision. She would even use that decision against him. When the argument came, it didn't last as long as Thutmoses feared, and none of the noble families ever knew about it.

Hatshepsut waited until they were alone. She was as casual as possible but it didn't make any difference. "I am going to bring Moses to the palace. He will be able to study the military arts with the other princes. I think I will take him and Beauty for rides at sunset like my grandfather did with me."

Thutmoses hesitated before he replied, "Won't that confuse the people? They all remember our father bringing out the babies wearing their small crowns."

"I intend for both of my children to rule when we are gone!"

"You know he is not your child. He is one of the Hebrew children. Do you intend to make a child of the slaves the Pharaoh of all Egypt? I kept your secret to save the child's life and yours, but this is ridiculous!"

"He is not a child of the slaves. He was given to me by Pepi. He has the soul of Amosis. I asked Pepi to go with me, and he led me to the child. Besides, how do you know that Thutmoses III is your son? He may be the son of Ramose."

"Better the son of an Egyptian than the son of a slave. At least he has royal blood. You said so yourself. Ramose could have been Pharaoh. Moses had to come from somewhere. He wasn't born in the Nile. Are you going to say that the stork put the soul of your grandfather or your great-grandfather in the slave's body? Everyone saw our father with the two children. They expect Thutmoses and Beauty to rule."

"He has Amosis' soul. Maybe the stork did carry it there. No matter what, Beauty will make the next Pharaoh! The one she chooses will be king. Our father was made Pharaoh by my mother. You became Pharaoh because of me. Beauty will choose. I am Pharaoh. My mother was a god. You don't understand anything. I bet one of the gods disguised himself as Thutmoses, and I was born."

Hatshepsut: The Pharaoh's Daughter

They never argued about the topic again. It was agreed Beauty would choose. The one she agreed to marry would be Pharaoh. It would be a while before she would choose. The princes were both treated well. Only a careful eye would see the extra encouragement given to the favored princes.

Secretly Hatshepsut planned to expand on the story that she was not the daughter of Thutmoses I, but rather the daughter of the gods. She decided that her mortuary temple would tell the whole story about how the god Amon loved her mother so much that he disguised himself in the form of her husband, Thutmoses I, and that she, Hatshepsut herself, was the result of that union. The belief in the miraculous nature of her birth would tell the populace that she carried the royal blood and not her husband even though he was also the son of Thutmoses I. When this story was widely known, it would be easy to explain the birth of Moses as the return of her beloved grandfather. She was sure that the people would love the story of her being given a child from the life-giving Nile.

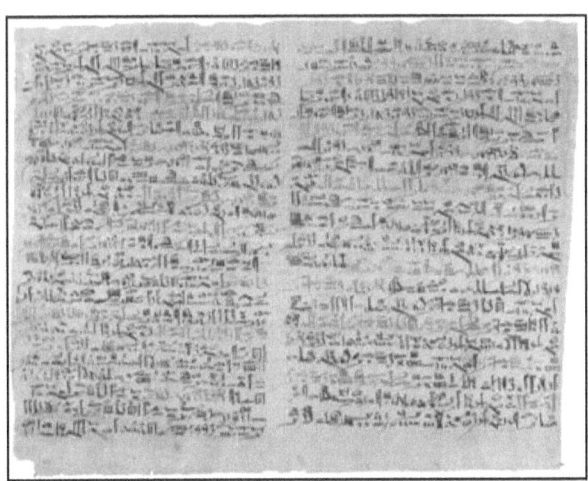

Papyrus that describes some Egyptian medical practices (Edwin Smith Papyrus)

Moses moved to the palace. Most mornings he participated in the military training with the sons of Isis. He learned quickly and the dexterity he had developed in the craft city helped him to develop into an accurate archer.

He did not neglect his former studies. The craft city was organized into ten-day periods. There were eight days of work followed by two days rest. Three of these cycles constituted a month. The annual calendar also included festival days. One workweek a each month, Moses continued his artistic and literary education in the craft city.

He, of course, stayed in the double house with Jocobed, who had by this time entrusted him with his true identity. He still called her "nurse" even when they were alone lest he be betrayed by his own voice. He had progressed to the study of the most ancient writing tables and immersed himself in the transcription of the literature of the Old Kingdom. He paid special attention to the work of the great Imhotep, the Hebrew Joseph. He learned what was known of medicine. He came to an understanding of the civil law that had ruled the land for centuries. There was no doubt about it; he was receiving as complete an education as anyone in the land.

One morning he came running into the house to tell Jocobed about his morning lessons. "Remember, nurse, how I have been learning how to carve and write all the signs for words? They have just showed us that we don't always write in full pictures for each word. There are a select number of words like house and ox that all have different first sounds. If those first sounds are memorized, they can be used to sound out any word. If we know those words then we, you know..." He paused to smile at her, expecting her to understand his excitement.

Jocobed nodded encouragingly, but was puzzled by the grin on her son's face. He continued, "Don't you see what it means? It means that we can write anything! We can even write the songs and lists of our own people. If the families are separated without the lists being learned, and we have written them down they won't be forgotten. You only have to learn that set of words, and you could write them! You know all the lists and stories. I could teach you."

"No my son, you will write them. My job is to take care of the princess and the queen."

"I don't have the time to do it either. Every day is busy, and I would have to do it away from all the other students."

"God will provide you with the time. Be patient. Just keep reciting them to yourself so that you can remember when He gives you the time."

Hatshepsut often brought Beauty to see her nurse even after she was weaned. In fact, they made a point of visiting several days when Moses was studying in the craft city. There was nothing the queen enjoyed more than sitting among her trusted friends, Senenmut, Jocobed, and the children. Senenmut took on the official role as tutor to the young princess. It was a role he had come to love as he had tutored Moses, Aaron, and Miriam. He continued to supervise all of Hatshepsut's building plans including the construction of the fleet.

Senenmut and Beauty

Sometimes they would sing as the sun went down. Sometimes they discussed the plans for the mortuary temple. One evening Beauty was sitting on Senenmut's lap listening to Miriam sing the song of creation; Hatshepsut said she would like to remember the scene forever. Senenmut suggested that Aaron carve a statue of Senenmut holding his youngest student. Together Aaron and Senenmut made a whole series of such images. They testify to the serenity of the child and the affection of the teacher for his pupil.

Hatshepsut Mortuary Temple (David Howe)

Hatshepsut especially liked to let her imagination go and describe her ideas in the presence of her friends. She was convinced that her mortuary temple at Deir El-Bahri was to be her most important work. She called it the Holy of Holies (Djeser-Djeseru.) The very name stirred her soul. She could see it in her mind. Visitors would ascend up the ramps that would be surrounded by beautiful gardens. The mountains in the background would add to its majesty. There needed to be plenty of room for stories to be plastered on all the walls. She was sure the gods themselves and the old Pharaohs who were made into gods would appreciate the tales as would any visitors to the site. A model of her temple was planned on the floor of the common room. Portico after portico would provide plenty of shaded space to document the history of her life and accomplishments. When Hatshepsut expressed concern that robbers might someday come to her tomb, she decided to make a secret tunnel back into the mountain where priests could hide mummies if the protection of the tombs became impossible. Senenmut said that his own tomb seemed shabby in comparison to her new one. He said he would like to build himself a second tomb to the side of Hatshepsut's. He felt no one would visit his old tomb once Hatshepsut's was finished.

The conversation was too much for Jocobed. She found herself singing the song of Job softly in the ear of the young Beauty, who at that time was nestled in her arms. "I know that my redeemer lives, and he shall stand at the last on the earth and though worms destroy this body yet in my flesh shall I see God." Then she spoke. "Do you not think that God can give you back your life even if your body is destroyed?" The Egyptians shook their heads. Where would the soul be placed if the body were gone? There would be no hope.

"What about all the people who cannot afford to build a tomb? What about those who are lost in sandstorms or at sea?"

"There is nothing we can do for them. We must make sure that a mummy is made for all we love. If this city is successful, more people will be able to have mummies made. Your father Joseph had his body made into a mummy. Everyone knows that."

"Yes, he made us swear on behalf of our children and our children's children that we would take his body back to our own land and bury him near Abraham, Isaac, and Jacob."

"There you have it! He knew he would need a mummy."

"No, he was making sure we knew that one day we would go home. God can make a new body for us as easily as he made the first one. We treat bodies with respect, but we don't put our hope in the preservation of the body."

Hatshepsut couldn't make sense of that statement so she changed the subject and turned to Senenmut. "When it comes to our boats, we have a problem. We want to sail the boats on the great water, but there is a desert between the water and us. It will be very hard to carry a boat big enough for the water over the desert. Do you think we could make them like puzzles that can be taken apart and put back together? Could we make pieces that fit perfectly? We make the fleet here. Then take each ship apart. Then carry the pieces by caravan to the sea. Fit the pieces back together. When the wood was placed in the water it will swell and the boat will be watertight. Of course the joints will have to be perfect, but everything we Egyptians do is perfect."

Senenmut thought quietly as if he could see the whole project in his mind. Then he spoke, "I don't think anyone has ever done that before but it might work. There would be more room for cargo than if we copied the boats of the other peoples. Let's try. If it does, then we could bury disassembled boats with the mummies just in case they need them in their journey in the next life. That would be the best use of all."

Jocobed laughed to herself. "They are still thinking about their bodies, their mummies."

Despite their differences, Hatshepsut and Thutmoses made a good team. They discussed strategy for keeping the nation moving forward. Lower Egypt was not neglected. Thutmoses made sure that the Northern palace was given an equal share of tribute money from the surrounding nations. Another center of learning had been established there. Monuments and buildings were also constructed. The structures of the more ancient Pharaohs were repaired as needed and stores of old tablets were excavated and transcribed for future study. A methodical plan for rotating the food stored in the store cities of Pithom and Ramses was established, and they were sure that no one would starve even if there were four or five years of poor crops.

Thutmoses, who had never excelled at war craft, now enjoyed going to the training areas accompanied by the two princes, Moses and Thutmoses, and the five other sons of Isis. What a sight they were. The Pharaoh always walked to the training area flanked by the two strong and handsome princes, and behind them came the five sons of Ramose. The people watched for them as they had the Sun-Chase of Hatshepsut and her grandfather. Each day they gossiped about how much the princes had grown. They didn't look like children anymore. The oldest sons were instructors, and they especially relished teaching their younger brother everything they knew. Moses was also a great favorite. He too was strong and appreciated any advice they were able to give him.

The princes learned to use the flail and staff of the Pharaoh. Moses was the older and stronger of the two and for many years the staff competition was a game where Moses taught the younger prince to hold the staff with his hands apart. They would hit their staffs together in a sort of dance. Moses would encourage the prince. "That's it! You're getting better." The younger boy wanted to be as good as the older ones and as he worked and grew, he improved. The day would come years later when the hitting and blocking came to an end with both princes lying down exhausted after a match. That would be the happiest day of the young Thutmoses life. It was the day he matched the other prince.

All the boys had mastered the composite bow. It required much more strength to use than a self-bow made from a single piece of wood. Its advantage was that it produced more force and distance. The Pharaoh himself finally mastered the skill along with the youngsters. Hatshepsut participated in the training as well though she did not attend every session.

There were days when her old fierceness showed itself and the princes watched not knowing what to think, but resolving never to cross her.

The successful training was just what the nation needed. Thutmoses was able to substitute courtly visits to the South and East for military campaigns. When the royal emissaries arrived accompanied with some of the princes, the monarchs agreed to continue tribute payments without objection.

Chapter 35:
Bees

As a young man Thutmoses had been afraid to go into battle. Once his skills were developed, he was no longer paralyzed by his fear. His mind often recalled the sacrifice of Ramose and confirmed his affection for the children of Isis. He didn't care if he were the father of the young prince or not. He was a fine strong boy. In the end it wasn't his fear that conquered him; his bravery won out. One fine day when the royal party was returning from the upper cataract, the strong boys decided they would rather walk than be confined to the boat. So it was that the royal party began the walk home. There was a road of sorts but it was largely overgrown, and everyone soon cut a switch to push aside the higher foliage as they walked along. The Pharaoh walked behind the boys basking in the memory that their appearance had made during the expedition. As if in celebration, he slashed with his switch at a log on the path even though there was no high grass to push aside. He hit a hive of bees that began to swarm. They came after him like a mighty army. They began stinging him. He gave a cry, turned, and ran away from the princes. The young soldiers turned and took in the scene. Moses cried, "Circle round among the trees; grab him and get him into the trees. Head for the densest growth; go quickly! Don't try to kill the bees; grab branches and cover your face. More branches! More branches! They won't be threatened by us if we disguise ourselves as trees!"

They executed the plan as if driven by a single mind. In a few moments they all lay still under some low hanging branches. Once the king and the others were covered in leaves, the bees retreated to protect their territory. Moses gave more orders, "Scratch any stingers away; don't squeeze them. It will put in more poison." The quick action saved the Pharaoh's life. They wove a litter of sorts to carry him to the palace. His face was covered with stings, his lips were swollen, and he began to vomit. The royal physician was sent for. Moses sent for the woman he called nurse.

The physician's verdict was grave. "Bees are the tears of Ra. You must have angered him. The bee is a symbol of Lower Egypt. Have you neglected your duty to your people there?" Thutmoses didn't know what to think; he had always tried to be fair in all his dealings with the people. Why would the gods send him this trouble?

Jocobed arrived with willow branches, a poultice containing some of the Nitrian salt, and some eucalyptus oil. She tore the bark from the branches and stirred the poultice with it and spread it on the stings, making sure that no stingers remained. After about a week the swelling subsided, but some of the bites were still visible. Some had become infected by scratching. He hadn't been able to eat much during the recovery, and his body looked like that of an old man. Jocobed and the physician agreed that if he were stung again it would probably be fatal.

Chapter 36:
Fear

Hatshepsut was afraid for the first time in her life. It would not be safe for Thutmoses to make any other excursions. It would just be too risky. Even the walk to the military complex was too far. There were flowers, which attracted bees, all along the way. One more sting and the body would swell up again. She had seen it happen before. If Pharaoh went out as usual, then he was in danger. If he stayed protected in the palace, then the people would imagine that he didn't have the will to defend the nation if it were attacked. The fleet of boats was nearly finished. The full-sized prototype had been carried out disassembled to the shore of the Red Sea and put together. It went together just as planned, and when it was dragged to the water the seams closed. It was time to send out the fleet. Who would go? She was willing to go herself, but could not leave the kingdom with only the viziers to keep order. Maybe the faithful Senenmut would be willing to go. He knew more than anyone about the construction of the seventy foot long ships, but he did not like to be away from home. He was a craftsman, not a diplomat. He would have to go. She would have to stay. If something happened to Thutmoses, what then? Both of the princes were too young to rule. There hadn't been enough time for the people to prefer Moses to Thutmoses. She liked both boys. The nation was more important than her own preference. After all their work to build up the nation, were they going to be brought down by a bee, a tear of Ra? She found herself crying out in her heart, "Pepi, help me. Pepi, help us! Show me the way."

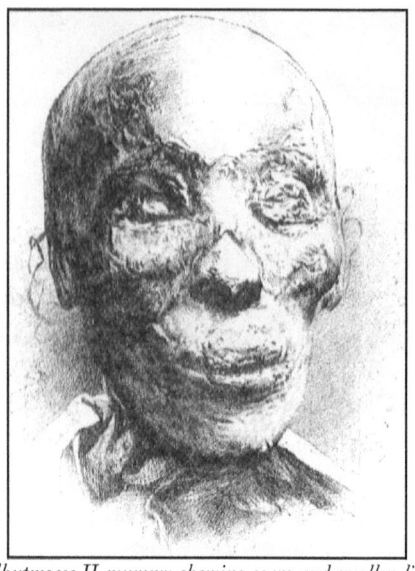

Thutmoses II mummy showing scars and swollen lips

The rumors began. The people were sure that the king was dying. He was never seen any more. Hatshepsut felt the country slipping away. Thutmoses was better; he needed to be seen. They decided that he could perhaps make the walk with the princes to the military complex to counter the people's anxiety. A couple of times each week he and Hatshepsut would accompany the trainees down the covered walkway to the military complex. Thutmoses spent the training time inside the storage building. The strategy seemed to work. The gossip lessened. People strained to catch a glimpse of him, and the royal headdress and decorative collar disguised the weakness of his body. Those who happened to see him would report to their friends, "Saw the king today; he looked pretty good."

It was too good to last. One day as the group made their way back to the palace, it happened. No one saw it coming. The king felt an impact on his forehead. He had walked directly into a beeline. One sting. That's all it took. He was able to walk for a while, but his lower lip began to swell before their eyes. The older sons of Isis supported him, and they made their way back to the palace. It didn't take long. The sting was removed but the swelling continued. His breath became raspy and then it stopped. His last words were "Hattie, Hattie, don't." He was gone.

Chapter 37:
Regency

The bad news traveled quickly. Within hours the local viziers were in the palace. Everyone had an opinion. The sentences were repeated over and over again.

"The boy is only eight."

"He's too young."

"There will have to be a regent until he is old enough." They took an informal vote and chose the eldest of their number. They thought there should be a succession of advisors, and they compiled an advisory list. They would send out the signal for an announcement from the portico to tell the people the official news that the king was dead and that Thutmoses III was the pharaoh, but that a regent would be announced within the week. When the people were assembled and the announcement about the Pharaoh's death was made, the unexpected happened. The people began to chant: "Pharaoh's daughter, Pharaoh's daughter, Pharaoh's daughter!" When they retreated to the palace, the viziers looked at each other and said, "The people have spoken." It was decided; Hatshepsut would be regent for the young Thutmoses III even as Ahmose, the Great Mother, had been regent for the good Amenhotep, her grandfather. There would be no objection from the people. It was the best decision. The people all loved her. Messengers were sent to the population centers and to the surrounding nations.

It didn't take long for the tribute nations to respond; they sent condolence representatives. When the first entourage arrived, Hatshepsut spoke to her attendants, "They are here to evaluate our strength." She sent for the military trainers. "I will bring the visitors to the complex in the morning. It is essential that they see strength and discipline everywhere they look. Put the best archers in chariots and have them hit targets. Have all the sparring centers filled. They must see soldiers, strong soldiers everywhere they look. Think of this as a battle. If they are impressed, we may avoid war in the future. Do you understand?" She ordered the princes and sons of Isis to the throne room. As she dressed she had an idea. She made her way to her husband's dressing room.

Egyptians did not grow beards and long hair. There was a constant battle against lice and heat. For formal occasions they wore wigs, false beards, and jeweled accessories. Hatshepsut intended to wear her husband's headpiece that symbolized the reign of both Upper and Lower Egypt. She viewed her image in the bronze mirror. She liked the effect. On impulse she reached for her husband's false beard woven with golden straps. She put it on. Then she took the ceremonial flail. It felt familiar to her hand. Hadn't she played with it as a child? She gave it a flick and laughed. She knew she would take them by surprise.

Even the princes looked surprised. They maintained their composure as she greeted the visitors. They bowed, but kept trying to look up to verify their first impression. She spoke first, "These are the royal sons. Thutmoses here is the crown prince, but I rule on his behalf until he is old enough to understand all the complexities of Egypt. These other men are also princes of Egypt. Thank you for your concern. We thought you would like to see where our young men spend most of their time. Follow me." She signaled to the princes to fall in beside her. She indicated that the guests should follow them. The muscular sons of Isis came behind them. The visitors felt a little intimidated by the tall soldiers behind them as they walked along the covered portico. When they arrived at the complex, Hatshepsut flicked the flail to indicate the various training sections. All the visitors declined the offer to spar with Moses.

Back at the palace a banquet awaited the guests. While they ate, the singers provided impressive entertainment. When the visitors returned to their own land, they reported that the new leader was a woman who was strong but unpredictable. She is surrounded by what appears to be an army of gods. When the story of her wearing a beard was told the reaction of the hearers included laughter, surprise, and fear. It may have been what Hatshepsut wanted. At any rate the tribute arrived in full and according to agreed upon times. Hatshepsut's performance worked so well she repeated it for other guests and even had some statues carved with the image of her wearing the attire of a Pharaoh.

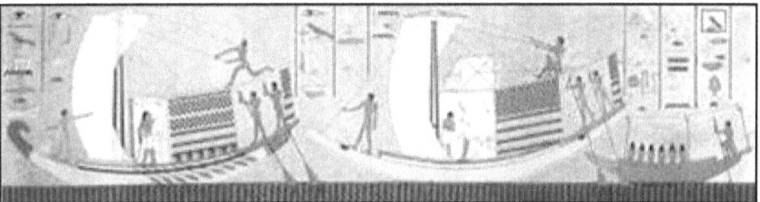

Egyptian Boats

Chapter 38:
Punt

Hatshepsut was still worried. The excursion with the five oceangoing ships needed to be made now. She would have Senenmut lead it. He would know how to deal with any problems during the voyage. If they could go and return before Thutmoses II's mummy was ready for burial, the viziers from all over the nation would witness the triumph of the project. The mortuary temple could record the accomplishment. If that building were ready for display, it would secure the national pride. She would consult with Senenmut immediately.

Senenmut and the chief treasurer led the expedition. There were five ships, each around seventy feet long, with over two hundred sailors on board. Each ship had thirty stations for rowers. It was an impressive sight. A regular trading route was established to the land of Punt. The ships returned with exotic animals, gold, incense, ebony, ivory, and a number of myrrh trees. Hatshepsut had the trees planted at her mortuary temple where she could casually say, "These trees were brought here over the ocean in our fleet of ships. You can read about the expedition on the walls of the portico over there." The tale did impress the Egyptian viziers and ambassadors from foreign countries as well.

Chapter 39:
Moses

Moses lived suspended between two worlds. He loved what he was learning from the Egyptians, but he knew his true identity. He knew many of the Israelites who worked in the craft village like his brother Aaron, but they thought him an Egyptian. The times when he could speak openly to his true mother were rare, but he was able to listen to her when the queen visited the craft city. Jocobed talked freely about her God. The Egyptians didn't mind. They had so many gods of their own; hers just seemed a curiosity. Moses hated seeing his people in slavery. His true mother was confident that God had spared his life not just for himself or for her, but for the good of all the Israelites. She knew God had promised Jacob that they would sojourn in Egypt for four hundred years, and soon that time would be up. She was sure that God had spared him for a special purpose. He was to be patient and watch to keep the temper of Levi under control. She had seen that temper revealed in herself, her husband, and even in her son. Most days he was able to think about his responsibilities to Egypt and take his mother's advice to wait.

Once Thutmoses was in his twenties, he began to approach Hatshepsut regularly to say that perhaps he was old enough to be Pharaoh. She always dismissed his suggestion saying that he still had much to learn. She answered him with a variety of excuses including, "Beauty will make you Pharaoh. She is the one who is from the gods."

"You and Moses are both princes."

"There will be plenty of time for you to rule when I am gone."

"I need you and Moses to protect our borders."

"You are both strong."

"We have not pressed our influence out since the time of your grandfather."

"I have something you need to do."

She sent Thutmoses and Moses to open up trade and influence even further to the East and South. Both princes proved themselves on the battlefield. It was almost a game between them. In time it stopped being a game and became a fierce competition. Thutmoses always wanted to be better than the older prince. When they returned from campaigns the soldiers reported stories of their valor and ingenuity. Hatshepsut had the campaigns recorded, and they were documented on steles throughout the country.

During each campaign Thutmoses dreamed that when he returned home victorious, Hatshepsut would relent and he would take his place as Pharaoh of all Egypt. Perhaps no prince ever coveted his birthright more. Every time she found more for him to accomplish or learn. His anger grew, but he dared not express it at all. He wanted to be rid of Moses so that he could have his throne.

Then one evening it happened. His heart's desire came true. Moses had been spending one of the eight-day cycles in the craft village. The evening was unusually cool so he thought he would walk to the constructions sites in the Valley of the Kings. As he went, he saw a small garden area in the distance. There were two figures. As he came closer, he saw that one of them was an older Israelite; the other an Egyptian. The Egyptian had a whip in his hand and was beating the old man. He was blaming the man for not producing enough food. Moses felt rage well up within him. He took his staff and challenged the oppressor who let out a laugh. "You! This man is just a slave; he will do what I say." Moses looked left and right, saw no one, and struck the man with one blow. He fell to the ground. The Israelite ran in the direction of the craft village. Moses dragged the body out into the desert and buried it in the sand.

The next day as he was walking through the village ready to make the return to the palace, he saw two Israelites fighting over a trowel. He said, "Why are you fighting?"

One of the men looked at him and said, "What? You, you Egyptian, you are not a ruler over us. Are you planning to kill me like you killed the Egyptian?"

Moses froze; the deed was known. He returned to the house of Jocobed and told her the whole story. She lowered her head and recited, "Cursed be the Levites anger, for it is fierce." Then she was quiet for a long time. When she spoke she was sure. "It was not murder; you did not lie in wait for the man. But this is just what Thutmoses needs to take power. Even the rumor of it will be enough. He will seek to have you arrested and put to death. There won't be a trial or anything. You are not completely innocent. Your lawful punishment would be confinement until the death of the ruler. You must leave Egypt. You must leave now. You will be in exile.

"Do not return to the palace. When Thutmoses hears of it, he will expect you to escape to the land of our fathers. He knows you have been there before on your expeditions. You must not go there. Leave a trail at first. Go North on the King's Highway but turn aside into the mountains where there are enough rocks that your footsteps cannot be seen. Midianites live there. They are shepherds. They worship the true God. After Abraham's wife Sarah died, he took a second wife named Keturah. The Midianites are their descendents. Thutmoses will not look for you among them. You will find a way to live. God will guide you. Do not return until Thutmoses himself dies. That will be the end of your punishment. When the time comes, Aaron will look for you there. Now Go! Every day Thutmoses hates you more and more." Then she smiled, " I think God is giving you the time you need to write down all our stories, songs, and lists. He will keep you. Go in peace." It was the last thing she said to him. Her comment took him by surprise. Writing was the last thing on his mind, but he did not object. She hugged him goodbye. In her heart she once again gave up her son to the will of God. Moses took some plain garments, food and water and left. He took a small boat as usual, but sailed past the palace. He did not try to hide the boat when he took to the path to the King's Highway.

When Moses didn't return to the palace, everyone thought he had decided to stay an extra night in the village. That was not unusual. When another night came and went, Hatshepsut became anxious. She crossed over to the West to see where he was. Jocobed reported that he had left on the eighth day as usual. Hatshepsut was afraid. The thought of treason crossed her mind, but she laid it aside. Then the servants began to hear the rumors of the murdered Egyptian who was buried in the sand. A search was made for the body, and the rumors were confirmed. By this time Moses had a head start of several days. Thutmoses volunteered for action. "I will find him and bring him back. I think I know where he will go."

Hatshepsut wanted Moses to come back home but was afraid of what would happen if he did. "Take some of your brothers with you. We don't need to lose you as well," she answered.

Moses was not found. There was no sign of him. Over the years Thutmoses took many campaigns North. Every time he searched in vain for his rival. While he was gone on the first of these raids, Hatshepsut finally relented. She knew she could no longer put off the marriage of the prince to Beauty. The rival for her daughter's hand was gone. She also hoped that Thutmoses would abandon the search for Moses when he became Pharaoh. So it was that Thutmoses III was crowned Pharaoh of all Egypt, and Hatshepsut was relegated to the position of advisor. When the wedding day arrived, the people were elated. The older citizens regaled the young people with the story of how Thutmoses I had stood so proudly on the palace portico with the two babies in his arms. More than one person commented, "It's about time!" Hatshepsut was content. If the people were happy, she would be happy. She was still a good ambassador for the nation, and the people always came out to greet her like a long lost family member. She completed her temple and continued some other building projects. Her daughter, Beauty, was now wife of Pharaoh, wife of the god. She longed to see Moses again, but she kept that to herself and was satisfied with the stability of Egypt.

The warrior Thutmoses III, shown defeating his enemies

Thutmoses became a very successful ruler. He was strong and powerful and admired by the people. They appreciated a ruler who led rather than one who just gave orders to others. He conducted over sixteen raids over a twenty-year period, pressing his forces as far as the Euphrates in the North and to the fourth cataract of the Nile in the South. Even when he was older, he still found himself searching for the figure of Moses in every battle. He never forgot, but he never found him either.

Back in Egypt he built over fifty temples. He increased the number of workers and continued the support of the craft city. The availability of skilled craftsmen made it possible for burial chambers to be built for the noble families and for the workers themselves. He built a forest of pillars to document the Egyptian achievements. He, too, raised obelisks to stand as a witness to his power. He did not remove those of Hatshepsut, but he carefully placed other structures to obscure their view. He continued trading using Hatshepsut's fleet of ships, astounding the nations with his ability to carry an oceangoing vessel overland to any port.

Life in the Wilderness

Chapter 40:

Mountains

Moses obeyed his mother and made his way into the mountains. His hair and beard grew, but his skills did not diminish. In the mountains he found a well. While he was resting there, the seven daughters of Jethro, the Midianite, came to water their father's flocks. A band of shepherds came along and drove away the animals of the women so they could water their own flocks first. Moved by the injustice of the scene, Moses sprang into action. He challenged the aggressors and single-handedly defeated the leaders, causing the others to retreat into the mountains. He then watered the flocks for the grateful women. When the story was told to Jethro, he encouraged Moses to travel with them. Eventually Moses became his son-in-law when he married Zipporah whose name means "Lady bird."

He certainly had a different life from the one he had in Egypt. Every day was a struggle to stay alive. No palace ceremonies. No palace bedroom. No permanent home. No secrets to keep. When he described his former life to his wife, he found it hard to believe himself. It seemed like a dream. He and Zipporah had two sons. The oldest he named Gershom whose name means "sojourner." By the time his second child was born, he felt more at home. He named him Eliezer or "God is help." His life in the wilderness mountains was utterly unconnected to the life that he had known. It is probable that if Thutmoses himself passed by Moses leading the flocks around the mountains, he would not recognize him in the least.

Moses was now a shepherd. The life was hard. The sheep provided clothing, meat, and leather. He soon mastered the skill needed to tan hides and then turn them into sandals, protective clothing, and tents. It didn't take him long to realize that scraps of the hides could be split and formed into parchment which could provide him with a good substitute for the papyrus he had used for writing back in Egypt. He laughed to himself and spoke out loud to his mother though she wasn't there. "Right again, mother! I have been given time to write and what I need to do it. How long will it take? Will you ever see them for yourself? Will I ever see you again?"

It wasn't going to be easy recording all the songs, stories, and clan lists of the people of God. He could only work when the flocks had abundant grazing territory, and they didn't have to be on the move. While he was driving the sheep, he had time to think about the extra task he had committed to complete. There would be no need to use the full Egyptian characters for the sounds of syllables. The people he was going to write for would never carve temple hieroglyphics. He could simplify them so they would be easier to write and easier to learn.

He saw that his first task was to design a simplified alphabet (actually an *Aleph, Beth, Gimel, Daleth, He*). He made a game of sorts with his sons. He would teach them to associate a symbol with sound. At first he drew a symbol with a stick in the dust, and they guessed the sound. When they got good at that, they reversed tasks. The boys took turns writing the symbols, and he guessed the sounds. They progressed to words, then sentences. Soon the boys could read.

Finally he began in earnest. The first thing he wrote on parchment was the song of creation. When he finished it, his sons read it back to him. Over the years he continued to write out selections on various pieces of parchment. He eventually sewed these together as a record of the Beginnings of the communication of God with man.

The ancient book of Job became his comfort in the wilderness. There were times when he was alone with the flocks that he wondered why he had spent so much time learning the ways of the Egyptians. Why had he learned all that? Was there a purpose in it all? He found solace and comfort in the writings of his God. He cried out for reasons. The book of Job expressed exactly what he felt.

"Oh that I knew where I could find Him! That I might come even to His throne! I would present my cause before Him...I would know the words which He would answer me, and understand what He would say to me. Will He argue against me with his great power? No; but He would put strength in me."

So often he prayed for that strength and asked God why he had been spared so miraculously. His mother had been so sure that God was preparing him for a great work. What was the work? Job seemed to have been there before him when he said: "Behold I go forward, but he is not there; and backward, but I cannot perceive him. On the left hand, where he works, but I cannot behold him. He hides himself on the right hand, that I cannot see Him: But He knows the way that I take and when He has tried me, I shall come forth as gold."

Was there a possibility that he, Moses, would come forth as gold? "God blessed the latter days of Job more than the beginning." Were these his latter days? Would there be another part to his life? He finally came to the conclusion that only God knew the answers to such questions.

Moses wandered all around the Sinai. He learned where water was to be found, where flocks could graze during various seasons, and where wadis would bring life flowing water to plants at certain times of the year. He worked on his manuscripts when he could, but sometimes thought he would run out of time. He might not even be able to finish. If he did, who would carry the manuscripts to his people? Who would teach them to read his new alphabet?

Chapter 41:
Passing

Back in Egypt Hatshepsut still lived in the palace. Thutmoses hated the fact that when he was gone he had to rely on her to conduct court and welcome visitors. He had to admit that there was no one better. He needed her, but he wished he did not. His wife was not as strong as her mother, but her beauty was breathtaking. He was sure that the dual impact of beauty and strength impressed emissaries. He always came home to a richer nation after each of his campaigns. For her part Hatshepsut did whatever she could for the benefit of Egypt. When Thutmoses was home, she spent most of her days in the craft city. She helped Jocobed with the little children. They loved her and still called her The Pharaoh's daughter. She took pleasure in seeing the skills being passed from one generation to another.

It couldn't last. The first sign of trouble began in the middle of the night. Hatshepsut's most faithful palace attendant woke to find a cat standing on her body. The moment she opened her eyes the cat let out a wail and jumped down to the floor. In the moonlight she could see the cat facing the door with her head turned to see if she were being followed. The good woman got up and obeyed. The cat trotted in front of her, turning back every few feet to see if the attendant was still there. They wound their way through the palace, down to the lower level, and outside to the kitchen area. There was Hatshepsut, sitting at a small table, eyes closed, hand to her head. In front of her was a steaming drink. She opened her eyes, looked up, and signaled for the servant to go away.

The servant obeyed and went back into the palace proper. She sought out the other attendants and related what had just happened. One of her friends said, "We need to send for the old nurse. She will talk to her." The others nodded agreement. The fastest messenger was entrusted with the mission. Jocobed came at once. The servants led her to the door that led to the outside kitchen area.

From the doorway she could see. The woman who had been Pharaoh sat holding the hot bowl next to her face. Her eyes were closed. The moment Jocobed entered, Hatshepsut again looked up. When she saw who it was, she began to cry and blurted out, "Oh nurse, the worm has broken through, it is eating my body. The pain! The pain! I am so tired but I cannot sleep! It hurts so much."

The faithful nurse went to the kitchen storehouse and returned with a small loaf of bread, a flask of wine, some salt, branches of white willow, and some small stick-like aromatic woody pieces. "Drink this." She handed her friend a cup of wine. She placed some salt in a bowl of water and heated it on the fire. When it was warm enough, she brought it back to Hatshepsut and said, "Hold some of this in your mouth and swish it around your tooth. Then spit it out. Do that a few times."

The woman obeyed. "Now bite down on this willow branch like you were making a brushing stick. Then squeeze it between your teeth and hold it tight there between your teeth. It is not a cure, but it will quiet the worm and give you some relief. You should be able to sleep some. When daylight comes, we will call for the royal physician."

When the pain subsided a little, a poultice of the bread was placed around the tooth and held in place by biting on the aromatic stick. The two women made their way to Hatsheput's chambers. Jocobed sang ever so softly to her friend, who finally relaxed and surrendered to sleep.

In the morning the physician came. He was surprised at the condition of the tooth. "It should have been removed before now; I am afraid it might shatter. It must come out." Hatshepsut squeezed tightly on her friend's arm as the physician extracted the tooth. As soon as it came out, a stream of blood and thick yellow fluid drained from the spot. The stream continued for several minutes. The pressure was released, and Hatshepsut felt completely relieved. She wasn't alarmed at all by the liquid that was being collected from her mouth. She just smiled with relief. The doctor signaled to Jocobed. The two went out of earshot of Hatshepsut and he explained. "The whole tooth did not come out. She will have several days without pain, but I'm afraid the worm is still there and it will attack her bones next. She needs to be prepared. You will need to have a supply of the herbs that will numb her senses. It will begin again. Be ready."

It was the hardest thing she ever had to do. It had been hard to place her son in the Nile, but then she had the greatest hope that the child would survive. Now she had to help the woman, who had saved her son, face her own death. It would have been easy to ignore the duty. Hatshepsut felt so much better. Why not give her a few days of peace? No, there might be things she needed to do. The physician had assured her that they knew how to minimize the pain but not the end result. Over the years the women had become friends; they understood one another, and they had the love of Moses and Beauty in common.

After the duty was done, Hatshepsut appealed to her friend, "Stay with me. I will not be afraid if you are with me. I am afraid of the journey after death. I know that you are not afraid. You have never been afraid. Will you stay with me then? You could be made into a mummy too and I won't be alone to face the gods. Please?"

"I am not afraid. You know that I believe I will be with God no matter what happens to my body. My body is just a temporary tent. God will make me a new one."

"When you die, let them make you into a mummy for me. Please. Don't leave me. Promise?"

Jocobed nodded. So it was decided. To Jocobed's surprise the first thing her friend wanted to do was to see the Pharaoh. She approached him with a respectful bow. "I have a request to make of you."

"What?" he replied.

"Swear, swear on your love for Egypt that when the nurse here dies that you will have her mummy made and that you will bury her in my tomb."

"Are you planning for her to die soon?"

"No. That is why I need your promise. I am the one who is about to die. Promise me. Swear on your love for Egypt."

It took a while for Thutmoses to comprehend the situation, but in the end he made the solemn vow. "It will be done."

The look of anxiety left Hatshepsut's face. A serenity she had never known overtook her.

The end was near. She knew it. She would use her last days well. That evening she took her grandson out in a chariot to chase the sun and tell the child the story of Tao the Brave. Why had she not done so before? She calmed herself with the thought, *He will remember this night.* The people remembered. On the way back home they were there as they had been when she was a girl. This time the flowers were handed to Amenhotep II, who had been named after her beloved Pepi.

The next day she walked through the temple complex to see once more the monuments she had caused to be raised. She laughed at the statues of herself wearing the beard. She could see in her mind the surprise on the faces of the visitors who had seen it in person. "That wasn't a bad idea. Was it,

Pepi?" She spent some time in the Red Chapel, which had been her favorite place for meditation. In the afternoon she visited the craft city, admiring the handwork of the young children and listening to the singing. She walked to her mortuary temple and read the inscriptions there. As she turned toward home she whispered softly, "See you soon, Pepi."

On the days that were left, the two women walked side by side along the Nile, watching the birds and boats, the tiny flowers and the palms waving in the gentle breeze. They were ruler and slave, but friends in life. Each sunrise and sunset was precious to the ruler, and her friendship with a slave turned out to be the most reliable of her life.

Hatshepsut's request had taken Thutmoses by surprise. She stood there looking well and asking for such a strange thing. Within days he understood. She was dying. The medications had been prepared to keep her comfortable, but they came with spells of delirium. A bed was made for Jocobed in her chambers. First came the fever. Then her mind began wandering: "Don't leave me!" "Where are you?" "Where is Moses?"

At times it sounded like a conversation, "Everything will be alright when Moses comes back, won't it?"

"Yes, everything will be alright when Moses comes back."

"Is he here yet? My beautiful boy?"

The medicine did its work and she slept. When she woke for the last time, she reached out to Jocobed. "I see him. I see Moses. He is coming this way. Do you see him?"

"No. I do not see him." The faithful nurse replied.

"He is telling me to come to him. He is calling to me."

"Go to him then."

"No! No! It's not him. It is not Moses. He is like him, very like him. He calls to me. He is so beautiful."

She sat up and reached out to the vision then fell back on her bed with peace at last. The race was over.

Jocobed washed the body and then relinquished it to the workers who would take it away to the West where her mummy would be prepared.

The people mourned. That evening as the sun began to set the people who lived along the sun-chase road came outside. Each one raised an arm to the sun as if in salute to their queen. "Good bye, princess, our Pharaoh's daughter." She was perhaps the most loved of all the Egyptian rulers.

Jocobed returned to the craft city where she continued to care for more children. The other women enjoyed her company and often sought her advice. She never forgot to recite the Sabbath prayers every seventh day. Those who were present in her house were tutored in the recitations of family lists after the celebration of each new moon. Her reputation for wise judgment grew and even the Egyptians came to her to settle disputes. They knew her decisions would be fair to all.

One day she arranged to meet with Aaron alone.

"What I am going to say to you now must not be repeated to anyone. Not even to Miriam. Pharaoh has promised that when I die my mummy will be made, and I will be buried with Moses' other mother. I too promised."

"But you don't believe in the Egyptian ways."

"Nevertheless I made a promise. Better to not promise than to promise and not pay. There is another promise you will have to fulfill. You must remember the promise that was made to Joseph that when the time came for us to go back to our own land, we were to take his mummy and bury it in near our fathers Abraham, Isaac and Jacob. The leader of each of the tribes knows the secret of his burial place; the knowledge has been passed from father to son all these years. The Egyptian priests do not know where it is. You must make sure that his body is taken home and that the promise is not forgotten.

"When Thutmoses dies, you are to go and find your brother. Head out toward the North; follow the King's Highway. When you see a path to the right that runs into the mountain wilderness, follow it. God will help you find him or have him find you. Once Thutmoses is gone it will be safe for him to return. God spared his life for a reason. I think he will use him to take our people home."

Hatshepsut had been right. Thutmoses still had years of rule ahead after she died. He became one of the most renowned of all the Pharaohs. He continued as a great builder, expanding the temple complex even more. He chose to be depicted as a great archer stretching a bow in battle. He was too superstitious to tear down Hatshepsut's obelisk, but he did not hesitate to build a wall around it. He did order that all of the likenesses of Hatshepsut and Moses be chiseled out so that there would be no remembrance of them. Her face was removed from the narrative sections of her tomb. His son continued the purging of her memory, but not everything was destroyed.

Jocobed's faith never wavered. She continued in thanksgiving to the end of her days, and when she lay dying, she sent messages to Pharaoh reminding him that he had promised Hatshepsut that she would be buried with her. Thutmoses kept his word. When the mummy was ready, he ordered that the body be thrown into the tomb with Hatshepsut. Then he added. "She wanted to be buried with her. Take Hatshepsut out of her coffin and let them both lie on the floor together." There their earthly remains rested for millennia. His own mummy did not stay in his tomb either. Dynasties later the priests found that looting of tombs was a real threat, and they removed the royal mummies to the secret cave that had been planned by Hatshepsut. The mummies of all the Pharaohs named Thutmoses were among those saved by her careful planning. Eventually Thutmoses' tomb was demolished in a landslide and even some of its foundations are gone.

Moses had spent the years of Thutmoses' reign protecting and tending the flocks of his father-in-law. His greatest work during his exile was the collection of scrolls he fashioned from scraps of leather on which he wrote down the stories of the beginnings of his people as well as the story of Job that his mother had taken such care for him to know.

There is a tradition that says that Amram, Jocobed's husband, who left her after the order to kill all boy babies, actually survived his slavery and was among those who became free when Moses returned. He spent his last days leading raiding expeditions into Egypt to recover bodies of Israelites and then bury them in the land of Abraham, Isaac, and Jacob. He is sometimes called Imran, a common name even today.

Senenmut did build a second tomb for himself near Hatshepsut's burial complex. This tomb was never used, and there is no trace of his body. The tomb containing the mummies of his mother and father have survived to modern times with all their artifacts intact. It is possible that he left Egypt to find a new life with his students who worshiped the unseen creator God.

Aaron practiced his crafts and mostly carved and painted letters in the Valley of the Kings. He fashioned metalwork and chiseled stone for the tomb of his friend Senenmut who loved him like a father. He carved beautifully and accurately all the while insisting that the true God needed no such provisions for his children for life after death.

Neferuer or "Beauty" listened to all the debate and to the singing of the Hebrew songs, and in the end she taught her children and grandchildren about the God, who cannot be seen, who is above all the gods, and who created the whole earth. Her words found their mark several generations later when the young Amenhotep whose body was twisted and deformed took comfort in the God who looked on the heart of a person, rather than external appearances. The young pharaoh changed his name to Akhenaton and wrote hymns of praise to the creator God.

When Thutmoses III died, Aaron kept his promise to his mother and sought his brother though he did not know where exactly to go. He turned aside from the King's Highway and headed up into the mountains.

It was at that time that God sent an angel in the form of the burning bush to attract Moses to the high spot above the road. God told Moses that the time had come to return to Egypt and tell Pharaoh to "Let my people go." When he protested that he couldn't speak to Pharaoh, God said, "Look, here comes your brother. He will be your spokesman." Moses looked down and saw his brother coming straight toward him.

In the years to come he used the wisdom that he learned as a prince in Egypt, but it was all transformed by his encounter with the God whose name is *I am* whom he met on the mountain. He did not make portable boats that could be taken apart and put back together as needed. He made a portable place of worship that was taken apart and put back together at each encampment in the wilderness. It also had a *Holy of Holies*, but it wasn't a resting place for a dried and shriveled body. It was the heart of a tent that symbolized living presence of God who had come to dwell in the midst of His people. Hatshepsut was right; all was well when Moses returned. Of course it took a while for the new Pharaoh to cooperate, but that is a different story.

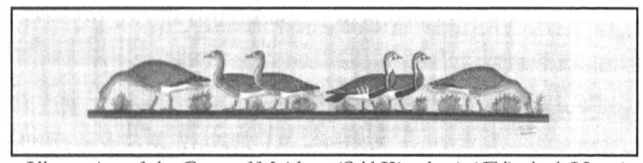

Illustration of the Geese of Meidum (Old Kingdom) (Elisabeth Howe)

The path of light across the night sky (Constance Baikie)

Acknowledgements

I have always been fascinated by Egypt and her history. When I was thirteen, my Scottish grandmother took me to see my first full color movie. It was *The Ten Commandments*. The first book I purchased when I was gainfully employed as a math teacher was *The Great Pyramid* by Peter Tomkins. That book gave me an appreciation of the greatness of the Egyptian culture and their scientific knowledge. During my seminary days I paid close attention to every reference to Egypt. In 1980 a whirlwind Bible Tour took my husband and me to Cairo, Memphis, and Luxor.

Meredith Kline, my Old Testament teacher at Gordon Conwell Theological Seminary, convinced me that the Pharaoh's daughter of the Bible was The Pharaoh's Daughter of Egypt named Hatshepsut. He had a Ph.D. in Assyriology and Egyptology and seemed to know the Patriarchs and other Biblical characters personally. He had an intimate knowledge of old Suzerain-Vassal treaties. An expert in ancient languages, he had been selected as one of the early translators of the books of Job and Psalms for the NIV translation. He laid out the evidence for the connection between Hatshepsut and Moses' deliverer. He convinced me. There is no other plausible alternative. Over the years I have read every article and book about the Pharaohs that crossed my path. I read about the condition of the various mummies of the Pharaohs and the speculation as to the cause of death for each one. Then in April, 2009, two years after the death of my teacher, *National Geographic Magazine* contained an article that described the apparent discovery of the mummy of the Pharaoh's daughter.

Hatshepsut: The Pharaoh's Daughter

Dr. Kline described Hatshepsut as a power-hungry manipulator who poisoned her husband, Thutmoses II, and terrorized her stepson, Thutmoses III, so that she could retain power. Her husband's mummy does show evidence of poisoning. She did hold power for a very long time as regent for Thutmoses III. Our 1980 trip took us to her reconstructed mortuary temple. The birth narrative carved there made me see her as a fascinating and imaginative individual. The Egyptian guide seemed to be extremely fond of her. The 2009 *National Geographic* article also indicated that Hatshepsut cared deeply about her people and that they in turn loved her. In my mind I tried to reconcile the two descriptions, the manipulator and the beloved woman who ruled Egypt for well over twenty years.

For years I have hoped that someone would write a historical novel about the connection between Hatshepsut and Moses. I finally came to the conclusion that I would have to write it myself. As I wrote, her personality came into focus in my mind. She was a strong, determined, imaginative, and loveable girl and woman. Hatshepsut has always been known as the Pharaoh's Daughter. It is time to see her as the Pharaoh's daughter you probably learned about as a child.

Illustrations by Constance Baikie come from a book entitled *Peeps at Many Lands.* It was written by her husband and published in 1912. Rev. Baikie's book is now in the public domain, and I have re-titled the illustrations in *Pharaoh's Daughter.* Most photographs were taken by my husband or daughter. Other illustrations are from public domain sources from before 1928 including the work of Karl Richard Lepsius (1810–1884) and *The History of Art in Ancient Egypt.*

The picture of Senenmut and Beauty is by Wikipedia contributor Captmondo under a Multi-license with GFDL and Creative Commons CC-BY-SA-2.5 and older versions (2.0 and 1.0).

About the Author

Hatshepsut, The Pharaoh's Daughter is Leslie Howe's first published novel. Born and raised in northeast Ohio, she now resides in Knoxville, Tennessee where she was recently named Teacher of the Year in recognition of her accomplishments as a teacher of mathematics. Her years in the classroom also led her to develop a complete line of software for the instruction of mathematical concepts as diverse as the symmetry of snowflakes to advanced calculus. Under the name Howe-Two Software, her programs are used in many high school computer labs.

Leslie's undergraduate degree is from Westminster College in Pennsylvania, and she also earned two master's degrees, one in mathematics from Cleveland State University and the other in theology from Gordon-Conwell Theological Seminary. In her spare time, she enjoys programming, writing books, and painting on porcelain. She and her husband, David, share a house with a dog named Ginger and a cat named Willow.